*Look what people are saying about
these talented authors*

### Vicki Lewis Thompson

"If you thought *Over Hexed* was phenomenal,
wait until you read *Wild & Hexy!*…
A rip-roaring good time."
—*Booklist*

"A sizzling setting…a delightfully cozy read
for a cold winter's night."
—*Romance Junkies* on *Nerd Gone Wild*

### Jill Shalvis

"Shalvis thoroughly engages readers."
—*Publishers Weekly*

"Witty, fun and sexy—the perfect romance!"
—*New York Times* bestselling author Lori Foster

### Rhonda Nelson

"This highly romantic tale is filled with
emotion and wonderful characters.
It's a heartwarming romance."
—*RT Book Reviews* on *Letters from Home*

"Wonderfully written and heart-stirring,
the story flies to a deeply satisfying ending."
—*RT Book Reviews* on *The Soldier*

## ABOUT THE AUTHORS

Writing romance is a dream job for *New York Times* bestseller **Vicki Lewis Thompson**. Where else could she get paid for falling in love with sexy men on a regular basis? She's published more than ninety books and has earned numerous accolades including the Romance Writers of America's highest honor, the Nora Roberts Lifetime Achievement Award. Her hot new series Sons of Chance debuts in June 2010.

*USA TODAY* bestselling author **Jill Shalvis** is happily writing her next book from her neck of the Sierras. You can find her romances wherever books are sold, or visit her humorous daily blog at www.jillshalvis.com, where she chronicles her I-Love-Lucy life.

A Waldenbooks bestselling author, past RITA® Award nominee and *RT Book Reviews* Reviewers' Choice nominee, **Rhonda Nelson** writes hot romantic comedy for the Harlequin Blaze line. With more than twenty-five published books to her credit and many more coming down the pike, she's thrilled with her career and enjoys dreaming up her characters and manipulating the worlds they live in. In addition to writing, she enjoys spending time with her husband, two adorable kids, a black Lab and a beautiful bichon frise that dogs her every step. She and her family make their chaotic but happy home in a small town in northern Alabama. She loves to hear from her readers, so be sure to check her out at www.readRhondaNelson.com.

# Vicki Lewis Thompson
# Jill Shalvis
# Rhonda Nelson

## BETTER NAUGHTY THAN NICE

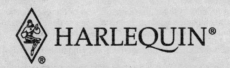

## HARLEQUIN®

TORONTO • NEW YORK • LONDON
AMSTERDAM • PARIS • SYDNEY • HAMBURG
STOCKHOLM • ATHENS • TOKYO • MILAN • MADRID
PRAGUE • WARSAW • BUDAPEST • AUCKLAND

Recycling programs
for this product may
not exist in your area.

ISBN-13: 978-0-373-79511-6

BETTER NAUGHTY THAN NICE
Copyright © 2009 by Harlequin Books S.A.

The publisher acknowledges the copyright holders of the
individual works as follows:

NO MISTLETOE REQUIRED
Copyright © 2009 by Vicki Lewis Thompson.

HER SECRET SANTA
Copyright © 2009 by Jill Shalvis.

SNUG IN HIS BED
Copyright © 2009 by Rhonda Nelson.

www.eHarlequin.com

**Printed in U.S.A.**

# CONTENTS

For Rhonda Nelson, who dreamed up
Damon Claus in the first place.

I cherish your warm heart...
and your twisted sense of humor.

# NO MISTLETOE REQUIRED
## Vicki Lewis Thompson

# Prologue

*CALLED ON the braided rug again*, Damon Claus thought, taking a smooth drag from the cigarette in his mouth. *Another year, another Christmas, another ass-chewing.* He blew a couple of blue-tinged smoke rings and smiled when they magically morphed into a pert pair of breasts.

"Stop that," his brother admonished from his arm chair positioned in front of the toasty fire. "The elves might see."

*Screw those little do-gooding green-garbed bastards,* Damon thought. He'd always hated them. It was bad enough being the brother to the most famous holiday figure in all of mankind—the big SC himself, *Santa Claus*—but constantly having the elves and their "commitment to the cause" rammed down his throat his entire life had created a bitter sense of resentment Damon was hard pressed to shake. He leaned against the mantle and idly rearranged the nutcrackers into lewd positions.

Muttering under his breath, Santa set his hot cocoa aside and lumbered up from his poofy chair. "Oh, for the love of mistletoe," his brother grumbled. He disentangled the little figurines and bent them upright again. "Damon, this has gone on long enough. You're a Claus—you're going to have to start acting like one. Let me bring you into the business," he implored for what felt like the hundredth time. "I'll put you in charge of the stables. You've always had a way with animals."

Damon snorted. A stable boy? A token post? He thought not. "Sorry, Tubs," Damon told him. "Not interested."

Santa's usually jolly face took a serious turn. "I figured as much. The only thing you seem to be interested in is thumbing your nose at family tradition and wreaking havoc during our busiest season. Christmas cheer has already taken a huge hit due to the rampant commercialism of our holiday, but you seem to delight in finding new ways to make people miserable. Stripping the ornaments from the tree in Times Square, busting up that Christmas parade—"

Damon grinned, remembering fondly. That had been some of his best work.

"Not to mention impersonating *me* and handing out condoms at FAO Schwarz."

"I was promoting safe sex," Damon argued, blinking innocently. He spied The List from the corner of his eye on the edge of his brother's desk and a new plan took hold. "What was the harm in that?"

Rather than respond, Santa merely looked heavenward as though summoning patience from a divine source. "I'm asking you, as my brother, not Santa Claus, to please, please, *please* refrain from your usual antics this year. According to the latest polls, more adults feel like Christmas is a burden than a joy and the number of children who don't believe in me anymore is depressingly low." Santa sighed, his giant belly threatening to pop the sash on his robe. He snagged a sugar cookie from a nearby tray. "Now more than ever, I really need you to behave."

Behave, Damon thought. Not truly be a part, not genuinely help. Just behave, he thought bitterly. It had always been this way. As the firstborn boy, Santa had inherited the primo Christmas position within the Claus family—the CEO, if you will—and Damon had always been cast as the bad seed. He'd misbehaved as a child to garner attention, then had fallen permanently into the role.

And, truthfully, he rather liked it.

He strolled over to the Christmas tree, smoothly slipping The List beneath his coat en route, and pretended to admire the newest ornament, a small snow globe featuring another picuresque Christmas scene.

"What do you say, Damon? Can you do it? Can you be good?"

Sure, Damon thought. He could be good…at being bad.

# 1

*DAMN, SHE'S STILL HOT.* Riley Kinnard gazed out the window of the airport van that had brought him from Tucson International to the house where he'd spent the first eighteen years of his life. Across the street, his former high school sweetheart was building a Christmas display in the yard, apparently ready to continue the tradition now that she'd bought the house from her folks. If he'd hoped to sort out his feelings before facing Hayden Manchester, he was out of luck.

Heading into the house without saying hello would be rude, not to mention cowardly. She knew he was coming home and had probably heard the shuttle, even though she continued wielding the hammer. As he climbed down from the van and walked around to the rear where his suitcase was stowed, he thought of what his mother had said on the phone. *It's a shame we've booked this cruise right when you've scheduled a job interview. But if there's a chance you're moving back, it doesn't matter so much. We'll tell Hayden not to bother with the mail. If you should accidentally lock yourself out, remember that she has a key.*

Of course she did. The Manchesters and the Kinnards had exchanged front-door keys thirty-five years ago when the subdivision was new. As a kid, Riley had been famous for locking himself out. Not Hayden. She did everything right. Near as Riley had ever been able to tell, Hayden was perfect.

She still was. Her glossy brown ponytail caught the afternoon sun as she raised one tanned, bare arm to bring the hammer down. Tall and athletic, she'd been a basketball star, a straight-A student, and his first love. Because Hayden had to lean over to wield the hammer, Riley had an excellent view of her ass encased in tight denim capris. Just like in high school, that sight made his jaw clench against a surge of desire.

When he'd first discovered that Hayden had left L.A. and bought her parents' house when they moved to Washington State, he hadn't thought much about it. He and Hayden were ancient history. But ancient history was looking way better than he remembered.

The shuttle driver hauled Riley's suitcase out and set it on the asphalt. Riley was so absorbed in watching Hayden that he nearly let the driver get away without a tip. At the last minute he fumbled with his wallet and handed the guy a five. Shortly thereafter, the shuttle pulled away.

As if waiting for that, Hayden gave the plywood one last whack with the hammer, straightened and turned toward Riley. She dangled the hammer from her right hand and adjusted her designer shades with her left. "So what, you got sick of Chicago?"

No conversational niceties for Hayden. Obviously, even though it had been ten years, she was still pissed at him. Yes, she'd caught him kissing Lisa Trenton the night of their high school graduation party. He'd been slightly drunk and very stupid, but Hayden had been completely unforgiving when he'd tried to explain.

He'd thought that heartache was healed. Maybe not. He pushed his Ray-Bans against the bridge of his nose. "Chicago's great but the winters suck."

"Could've told you that." She swung the hammer idly by her side

He laughed. Nothing had changed. Hayden still knew everything. "The work experience was awesome, but after five winters of ice and snow, I'm done. Speaking of relocation, what's a Hollywood set designer doing back in Tucson?" He was trying mightily not to ogle her chest.

She'd tied a carpenter's apron around her waist, which pulled her black tank top tight over her breasts. The shirt advertised the movie *Transformers,* and mechanical monsters had never looked so good. Hers were the first breasts he'd ever touched, and seeing them showcased in that snug tank shot him right back to his hormone-laden teen years.

"I travel for the job, anyway, so I decided I'd rather be based here than in L.A. My dad got a great job offer in Washington and they decided to move." She shrugged, which made her breasts shift invitingly. "I didn't want strangers living in my childhood home."

God, she was magnificent. With her high cheekbones and expressive mouth she could have been a model if she'd chosen that path.

He moved toward her without planning it, feeling a lot like an X-wing fighter caught in a Death Star tractor beam. "Yeah, that would be weird, not having Manchesters in that house." So she still had a sentimental streak. He wondered how sentimental she was about her old high school sweetheart. Probably not very, considering how they'd ended things, with her calling him a faithless bastard and him calling her a cold-hearted bitch.

He wished she'd take off the sunglasses. He'd always been able to tell a lot by looking into those big brown eyes. During sex they turned positively luminous with joy. But the last time he'd looked into them—had it really been ten years ago?—he'd seen nothing but the flames of fury.

Well, he sure as hell wasn't going to mention that incident. She'd been so sure of his guilt back then, and age hadn't seemed to soften her any. He didn't need to get hung up again on someone who was so quick to judge. Her unbending behavior still rankled, even now.

Shoving those feelings back into the box where he'd kept them for years, he gestured toward the structure she was building. "I see you're keeping up the tradition."

"Well, yeah." She glanced back at her work. "Mom and Dad are flying down on Christmas Eve day, and I couldn't let the front yard go undecorated, even if your parents aren't into it anymore."

"They told me they weren't doing much this year." Riley had been so involved with Hayden that he hadn't yet noticed his parents' home. Now that she'd mentioned it, he had to admit the place looked forlorn with nothing but three spiral white-light trees grouped on the lawn.

Not many places in Tucson had lawns anymore, with most people opting for cactus and gravel landscaping. The Manchesters and the Kinnards had kept the grass because it gave them the best base for their elaborate holiday constructions.

In times past, the Manchester-Kinnard Christmas decoration rivalry had reached epic proportions. The year Riley and Hayden were seniors, the Manchesters imported live animals for their nativity scene, and the Kinnards responded by getting the football team, including Riley, to dress up as tin soldiers and march around the yard with the Nutcracker Suite blaring. Cars lined up bumper-to-bumper on their street that holiday, and the rivalry ended up on the KGUN evening news.

Riley took stock of what Hayden had built so far. "Is that a bunkhouse?"

"Exactly. I'm going retro, Christmas in the Old West."

"Good idea. Shouldn't be too hard."

Her chin lifted defiantly. "That depends on how it's done."

If he didn't know better, he'd swear he just heard a gauntlet hit the ground. He wasn't picking it up. He had job interviews this week which he intended to ace so he could move back to sunny Tucson. His parents seemed happy with their spiral trees, which would look considerably better at night.

He smiled sweetly. "Knowing you, it'll be done perfectly." He might have allowed a trace of sarcasm into that remark. Old habits died hard.

"I plan on it."

From across the street, a V-8 revved up, causing Riley to look over and realize that his suitcase sat in the path of the oft-restored red Mustang backing out of his next-door neighbor's driveway. David Faulkner loved that car with a passion but he was the worst driver in the history of automobiles. He'd wrecked the Mustang more times than anyone could count. He'd once failed to notice a garbage truck when he backed out, so it was a solid bet he'd never see Riley's suitcase.

"'Scuse me." Riley sprinted across the street and snatched the suitcase out of the way just in time.

David slammed on the brakes. "Riley Kinnard! Your mother said you'd be in town this week. Welcome home!"

"Thanks, Mr. Faulkner." Riley noticed that his neighbor had a little gray going on at his temples and a few more laugh lines around his blue eyes, but otherwise he looked the same—great smile, wire-rimmed glasses, a lanky body that never seemed to gain weight. He and his wife both taught at the university.

"Hey, Riley, I'm only fifteen years older than you. Feel free to call me David so I don't feel like such a relic."

"Okay, sure." Riley wondered if he could do it. The Faulkners had moved into the house as newlyweds when Riley was seven. Childless themselves, they'd spoiled the neighborhood kids rotten. Riley's parents had instructed him to call all adults by their last names, even if he knew their first names perfectly well, and that included the Faulkners.

"Listen, I'm sure your mom left you a refrigerator full of food," David said, "but Marlena and I would love to have you over for a meal while you're here."

"I'd love it." Riley had been hoping for an invite. Unless

things had changed, the Faulkners put on an amazing spread. David's beer bread was legendary.

David leaned out of the car window and called over to Hayden. "You should come, too! Marlena hasn't finished pumping you about the stars you've met. How about tonight?"

Hayden hesitated just long enough for Riley to know she'd rather have a root canal than spend an evening with him. Apparently she held a grudge. What the hell, so did he. She'd broken his heart, which was a big deal when you were eighteen and in love for the first time. Or in lust. They'd had lots of sex their senior year, and great sex tended to blur the love/lust debate, especially at eighteen.

"I sort of had plans," Hayden said.

David flashed her a smile. "I have a slice of cheesecake with your name on it."

Hayden smiled back. "You know I can't resist your cheesecake. I'll cancel what I had scheduled. What can I bring?"

"Salacious stories about famous people. A night with you is better than an issue of *The Enquirer.*"

Riley hadn't realized how much he'd wanted the evening to pan out until Hayden agreed to show up. He tried to convince himself his eagerness was all about nostalgia. His sister Ginny was eight years older, so he'd spent much of his early years running around the neighborhood with Hayden, who had no siblings. They'd scrounged scrap lumber to build forts in the desert, a desert that had since become a series of housing developments.

He credited those forts with inspiring his career as an architect. He wondered if they'd steered Hayden in the direction of movie set design. He'd never asked, but he'd like to. The Faulkners might provide a DMZ where he and Hayden could talk without sniping at each other or dredging up painful memories.

"Let's say six." David gave them each a wave before careening out onto the street and zooming off, tires squealing.

Riley shook his head. Even as a teenager, he'd never driven like that. But in a way, it was comforting to come home and discover David Faulkner continued to be a maniac behind the wheel and Hayden Manchester was determined to decorate her parents' front yard for the holidays. If he had any community spirit, he'd—nah. That was nuts. Just because he was already envisioning a plywood representation of the Chicago skyline with Santa's sleigh flying overhead didn't mean he had to do anything about it.

*DAMN, HE WAS STILL HOT.* Hayden gave Riley a dismissive wave and returned to her construction zone as if he were no more than a minor interruption to her day. But inside, where Riley couldn't see, she was a mass of hormonal urges. If she'd had some vain hope that he'd gone bald or developed a paunch, that hope was dashed the minute he'd stepped out of the van.

Eyeing him while pretending to continue with her hammering hadn't been easy, but in Hollywood a person developed those skills. Celebrities were everywhere in L.A., and yet no one wanted to be caught looking. That would be totally uncool. So Hayden had perfected the art of watching without seeming to pay any attention at all.

Therefore she'd been completely aware of how great he looked in his jeans, dress shirt open at the neck, and black leather jacket. A guy like Riley, with football-star shoulders and narrow hips, could really pull off a combo like that. His hair was dark and thick, the way it had been when she used to bury her hands in it while he'd been deep inside her. Even though he'd kept his shades on today, she could easily recall the emerald green of his eyes.

Lying eyes, as it turned out. She'd been so sure of him, and then she'd caught him kissing Lisa Trenton and copping a feel, no less. Hayden had hidden her pain behind a wall of anger. How could he? She'd given him her virginity, and then she'd given him complete access to her body during their hot sessions in the back of his pickup.

She blushed to think of all the things she'd allowed under those starry desert skies. At a used bookstore he'd found a copy of *The Joy of Sex* and had coaxed her to try all sorts of positions. He'd also initiated her into the wonders of oral sex. True, she'd loved every minute of their experimentation and she'd soon begun paging through the book looking for ideas of her own.

They'd planned to enjoy another night of fun and games once they'd put in a token appearance at various graduation parties. Unfortunately, one of those appearances had involved a lip-lock and a grope with Lisa. Hayden had felt so deeply betrayed she'd barely been able to talk. But she'd made her point eventually—she and Riley were through. Over. Finished.

He'd tried to make some sort of lame excuse that Lisa had been the one to start it, but the sight of his mouth, which had been everywhere on her body, pressed hard against Lisa's mouth, plus the sight of his hand where it had no business being…that had been the ultimate insult. Hayden hadn't been able to get past it then, and she got cold chills when she thought about it now.

Not that she'd pined for him for ten years. Hollywood had its share of good-looking men, and she'd enjoyed herself. But no matter how hot the sex, she hadn't been able to recapture the sense of rightness she'd felt with Riley. She'd discovered a girl couldn't talk herself into being in love, and God knows she'd tried.

At times she wondered if Riley's betrayal had ruined her for finding true love. Other times she'd laugh at the notion as being way too melodramatic. After all, they'd been kids. It shouldn't mean so much. But seeing him again today, she had to admit it meant a whole hell of a lot. Damn him.

Swinging the hammer with a vengeance, she missed the

nail and hit her thumb hard enough to raise a blood blister. A string of swear words followed. She berated herself for not wearing gloves as she hurried into the house in search of the first aid kit. She hadn't worn gloves because the only ones available were ugly and she'd wanted to look cute when Riley arrived. The carpenter's apron was dorky enough, but she needed it to hold the nails.

She shouldn't have cared whether she looked cute or not. So what if Riley was interviewing for jobs and might be moving back? He wasn't interested in her, that was for sure. If he had been, he would have tried harder to make up after she ditched him. Instead he'd gotten mad at her, which made no sense considering he was the offending party.

She needed to forget about that, though, and put him completely out of her mind. But how could she, when she'd just agreed to have dinner with him over at the Faulkners? Well, she'd just have to think of it as a night at the Faulkners and ignore the fact Riley would be there.

Even so, she needed to look good while she was ignoring him. Smoothing a bandage over her thumb, she walked into the master bedroom, now hers, and opened the closet. Thanks to years of hanging out with costume designers, she had some awesome clothes. Riley might show up at the Faulkners in jeans, but she didn't plan to. *Eat your heart out, Riley Kinnard.*

RILEY'S BEDROOM no longer looked the way it had when he'd lived there. Gone were the wooden bunk beds where he'd had countless sleepovers with his buddies. Gone were the F-16 models that used to hang from the ceiling, and the Red Hot Chili Pepper concert posters that had decorated the walls.

His CD player had long since died, and so had the small TV he'd been so proud of. Still, he had a bedroom to come home to. Ginny hadn't fared as well. Her former bedroom was now a home office for his mom's real estate business.

In his old room, a queen bed sporting a pastel flowered comforter took up a good part of the space, along with bedside tables in walnut topped with wrought iron lamps, and a leather easy chair in the corner where he'd had his drafting table. A walnut TV cabinet had replaced the bookcase that Riley had covered with spilled model paint and globs of dried glue. Nothing much remained of him in this room, except the slight discoloration on the closet door.

He put down his suitcase and walked over to run his finger over the muted stains. The memory made him smile. At the age of ten, he and Hayden had collaborated on a model of the *USS Arizona* to enter in the Pima County Fair.

Predictably, they'd fought over who would apply the decals. He'd called her a dumb girl who didn't know anything about destroyers and she'd thrown a bottle of black enamel at him. He'd ducked, and the bottle had hit the closet door with enough force to break.

They'd both been in a pile of trouble over that, him for being disrespectful and her for being destructive. They'd paid for cleaning the carpet out of their allowances, but the door had soaked up too much paint to get it all out.

Under his mother's supervision, they'd divided up the decals and put them on. The model had won a blue ribbon, and they'd traded off the ribbon and the model every month for two years, until he'd finally given them both to Hayden to keep. He wondered where that model and ribbon were, now.

Maybe he'd ask her about that tonight at dinner. If she still had them and didn't want them, he'd take them back. He would have kids some day, and they might be interested in—

The doorbell interrupted his thoughts. Maybe Hayden was coming over to borrow a cup of sugar. Yeah, right. Not likely. He walked back down the hall and through the living room.

His parents had put up an artificial tree, which was another break from tradition. They'd always bought a live tree in the past. This one looked okay, but it had no smell, and Riley loved the scent of evergreen.

Stepping into the foyer, he opened the door, still halfway hoping to see Hayden on the other side. Only it definitely wasn't Hayden.

The guy on the other side was drenched in attitude, from his mirrored shades to the tattoos on his biceps. He was the sort who went to a gym primarily to meet chicks by showing off on the weight machines. The T-shirt tucked into his well-worn jeans sported the slogan Deck the Halls With Damon Claus. Underneath that was a stencil of two red Christmas balls.

"Season's greetings." The man flashed a smile. "I'm here to help you."

"With what?"

"Damon Claus, at your service. I specialize in exterior holiday decorations, but I'm available to consult on interior decorations, too. Our company motto is We Create, You Celebrate." He pulled a card out of his hip pocket and waggled it in front of Riley.

"I appreciate the thought, but this isn't my house. I'm staying here temporarily, and the owners are out of town. Any decorating decisions are up to them."

"So who put up the three trees?"

"Uh…" Living in apartments for years had blunted Riley's talent for getting rid of unwanted salesmen. Besides, the guy was talking about a subject that had been bugging him ever since he'd arrived—the lame decorations his parents had settled on.

"The thing is, I don't mean to poke fun at the trees, but this place could use some serious upgrading. Especially considering what's going on across the street." He jerked a thumb over his shoulder. "There's major holiday hustle over there."

Riley could hear the buzz of a power saw coming from

the Manchester's open garage. "I know. They always have a big display."

"Word on the street is that this house usually does it up pretty good, too. I'm doing some work for your neighbors, the Faulkners, and they told me about a thirty-year-old rivalry between this house and that one. Looks like that rivalry's DOA, man. Which is too bad, because that's what's made this country great."

Riley stared at him. "Christmas decorations?"

"Hell, no. Competition. Gets your blood pumping, your creative juices flowing, your pecker—"

"I need to interrupt you, Mr. Claus, if that's your real name."

"Trust me, I wouldn't make up a name like that. Sometimes I wish it wasn't my name, but what can a guy do?"

"I suppose you go into the Christmas decorating business. But I'm not going to hire you. If my parents want to stick with three spiral trees, then that's what we'll have out there." He winced. He hadn't meant to reveal that the house belonged to his folks. A person shouldn't give a persistent salesman extra information. Belatedly he remembered that.

"Ah, your parents." Damon Claus nodded and looked wise. "Don't wanna rock the boat, cause hard feelings."

"It's not that." Riley's irritation increased. "If I wanted to throw myself into the decorating thing, I'm sure they'd be fine with it, but—"

"Then do it! Thirty years of tradition is on the line! Your neighbors are expecting a show!"

"I don't care what they're expecting. I'm here to interview for a job, not put up Christmas decorations."

"That's where I come in. I can erect a display that will knock your eyes out. You'll be the envy of the whole street."

"Thanks, but no thanks."

"Okay, okay." Claus lifted his hands in surrender. "She told me you'd say that, but I had to try."

"Who told you?"

"The babe across the street, the one putting up such a righteous display. She said you probably wouldn't care about any of it."

"You talked to her?"

"Sure, I talked to her. But she wants to do her own, and I respect that. I talked to everybody on the block. A few hired me, but they all said the same thing—Christmas won't feel the same if the Kinnards wimp out this year."

Riley could deal with the rest of the neighbors being disappointed. But Hayden's assumption that he wouldn't care about the decorations galled him. He cared, but he was honoring his parents' wishes.

*Cop-out!* yelled his conscience. *Your parents might love having you take over the Christmas decorating this year. They didn't feel up to it themselves, but they would love coming home to a display worthy of the Kinnard tradition, especially if it was engineered by their son.*

"I'll be going," Claus said. "See you around." He started down the curved walkway toward his truck.

"Wait."

Claus stopped in his tracks. No doubt he had a triumphant smile on his face, but if so, he'd wiped it off by the time he turned around. "Second thoughts?"

"Yeah."

"Excellent."

Riley rubbed the back of his neck. He had to be insane to consider this, but he couldn't stand by and let Hayden assume he'd lost his competitive edge. Matter of fact, with a degree in architectural design and five years with a prestigious Chicago firm, he could decorate the hell out of Christmas.

He'd chafed at the bit lately watching his parents' efforts, which had become more routine than inspired. But he hadn't been here to help, so he hadn't been able to say anything.

He was here now and Miss Hollywood set designer could eat his dust. "I don't have time to get materials, but I can sketch out what I have in mind. If you bring what I need, we can work together to put it up."

"I'm your guy."

Riley didn't have a ton of confidence in Claus, but the job would require some help, especially with the interviews he had scheduled. "Come on in." He stepped away from the door. "We'll work out the details."

As Claus strolled through the door, Riley glanced across the street and noticed Hayden had stopped working to gaze at him. Instinctively, he raised his hand, forefinger extended. It was the signal that had fueled the Christmas decorating rivalry between the two families for thirty years. *We're number one!*

Hayden responded with an identical gesture. The battle was on.

# 2

HAYDEN HAD TO LAUGH at herself. First she'd returned Riley's ridiculous hand signal, and then she'd spent far too much time getting ready for dinner at the Faulkners' house. Sure, she wanted to set Riley back on his heels, but the amount of time she'd put into the project was obscene.

She'd knocked off early from her Christmas construction work to give herself both a manicure and a pedicure. She justified the pedicure because she'd decided to wear peep-toe pumps with her black dress. She chose Santa-Suit Red for her fingers and toes. The jersey dress clung in all the right places, but the skirt was a conservative length and swished demurely around her knees when she walked.

There was nothing overtly sexy about the outfit, especially with her understated silver necklace and hoop earrings, unless a person noticed the low-cut neckline, which she figured Riley would. Once upon a time she'd have worn a dress like this in anticipation of Riley taking it off. Tonight he could eat his heart out.

She'd washed her shoulder-length hair and used a curling iron so it softly framed her face. A quick twirl in front of the mirror convinced her she had a good chance of succeeding in her goal—to make all Riley's blood drain south.

Grabbing an ivory swing coat from the closet, she tucked her house key in the pocket and walked out her front door at five minutes before six. The Christmas lights in neighboring yards added splashes of color to the deepening twilight. Hayden hadn't hooked up any lights yet, and she wouldn't until she'd finished her construction. She had a specific mood in mind, and she didn't want to spoil it with premature lighting.

Until this afternoon, her yard decoration scheme had been for the fun of continuing the tradition and the satisfaction of surprising her mom and dad when they arrived on Christmas Eve. But ever since Riley had invited Damon Claus into his home, ever since Riley had saluted her with the gesture they'd used so often to signal the beginning of any competition between them, her motivation had changed.

As kids, they'd tried to best each other at everything under the sun, from video games to sports. Even after they'd started dating, the rivalry hadn't died. In some ways it had intensified, fueled by hormones. They'd battled for hours on the tennis courts and she'd held her own shooting hoops in whichever driveway they happened to choose.

Previously, the Christmas competition had been a family thing rather than a contest specifically between Hayden and Riley, but they'd each done their part there, too. Now it was strictly between the two of them, and just like the old days, she was out to beat his ass.

Enticing smells of onions and garlic wafted from the Faulkners' neat ranch-style house as Hayden walked up the flagstone path. Marlena had set out pots of petunias and pansies to liven up a yard that was dominated by prickly pear cactus and a large saguaro. A Christmas wreath hung on the carved wooden door, but there were no other outdoor decorations yet.

Damon Claus had told her that the Faulkners had hired him to string lights on the cactus, which was a job David had struggled with in years past, often drawing blood in the process. But he'd persevered because traditionally everyone on the block put up something for the holidays, and they all took pride in the combined effect. Hayden loved living here for many reasons, including the sense of community. She knew most of her neighbors, and that was a good feeling.

She'd known one particular neighbor a little too well, and she would have preferred that he stay in Chicago. She couldn't blame him for wanting to move back to Tucson, though, and even if he relocated here, he wouldn't be living across the street. With the salary he was rumored to command, he might buy a house in the foothills.

Come to think of it, he might have a girlfriend who would make the move with him. Hayden hadn't really thought about that. Well, so what? She didn't care if he came back to town with a gorgeous woman in tow. Her days of worrying about who Riley kissed were over.

Or so she tried to tell herself as she rang the doorbell and discovered her heart was beating much faster than it should have been considering she'd only walked across the street. Dressing up for Riley must have kick-started her libido, because she seemed to be thinking about Riley's mouth way too much.

David opened the door wearing corduroy pants and a sweatshirt with Christmas elves on it. "Hayden! Punctual, as always."

"I can't help it, David." Right after she'd moved into her parents' old house, he'd made the same speech to her about first names that he'd given Riley today, but she still had to think about it whenever she saw him. "I'm always the first one to arrive."

"Not this time." David stepped back and ushered her inside. "Riley showed up at least a half-hour ago. He's back in the kitchen helping Marlena make the salad."

"He came early? But—"

"I know. Riley used to be late to everything, but I think the boy's grown up some." He took her coat. "It's great to have the two of you here again. Like old times."

Hayden caught a gleam in David's eyes, and she didn't

think it was a reflection from his glasses, either. "Well, not exactly like old times," she said.

David leaned toward her and lowered his voice. "No girl-friend. I asked."

"And I care about this why?"

"Because in all these years, neither one of you got married. I think there's a reason for that." He wiggled his eyebrows.

"Of course there's a reason. People in their twenties are too busy building a career to think about marriage. I'm sure you've noticed that down at the U of A."

"I guess." He hung her coat in the closet by the front door. "But by my calculations, you're about to exit your twenties, and your career is in fine shape."

"If you're playing matchmaker, forget it."

He glanced at her dress and grinned. "Riley's stylin' to-night, too. Green silk shirt that looks designer to me. I guess the two of you got all dressed up to impress Marlena and me. I'm honored."

*Caught.* And worse yet, Riley was playing the same game. "We used to go out together. A girl always wants to look her best when she sees an old boyfriend. It's not as if—"

"David!" Marlena called from the kitchen. "Bring Hayden on back. The appetizers are done and I need you to open the wine."

"Coming!" David swept his hand in the direction of the kitchen. "After you, Miss I'm-not-interested."

"I'm not." She walked through the living room, which hadn't changed much at all since her childhood except for the added souvenirs on the walls and the bookshelves. The Faulkners were great travelers and would rather take a trip than buy a new sofa.

"If you say so." David followed her.

Hayden entered the fragrant kitchen as Marlena, a short, curvy woman with red hair and freckles, pulled a cookie sheet filled with baked hors d'oeuvres out of the top oven. The lower oven—the Faulkner meals usually required both to be used—contained a roasting pan of beef stew, if Hayden's nose was giving her the right info.

There should be a law against a scene like this. Not only did the kitchen smell like heaven, but a Greek god in a moss green shirt stood at the counter slicing radishes on a wooden cutting board. It wasn't a stretch to imagine that marriage to Riley could be exactly this wonderful.

Well, maybe not quite. Unless Riley had *really* changed, he couldn't cook worth a lick, and neither could she. They'd have to hire the Faulkners to complete the picture.

Riley glanced up. "Hi, Hayden."

"Hi, Riley." As she'd figured, the shirt matched his eyes. No fair. Nobody should look that good slicing radishes. Or be so accomplished at it that he could continue to smile at her and use a knife at the same time.

"Ouch! Shit!" Riley jerked his hand back from the cutting board and stuck his finger in his mouth.

Marlena set down the cookie sheet and turned to him. "Riley, did you cut yourself?"

"Yeah." He stared at his finger, which was still bleeding. "Got a bandage?"

"I'll get one." David left the kitchen.

Hayden curbed her instinctive urge to offer sympathy. Partly because they were both so damned competitive, they'd suffered through many scrapes, cuts and bruises together. She'd broken her arm on a fall from her bike and he'd kept her courage up as they'd walked all the way back home. His years on the high school football team had been agony for her, and the night he'd dislocated his shoulder had been pure hell.

But a cut finger was hardly in that league. Besides, those days were over.

"I'm so sorry." Marlena ripped a paper towel from the holder mounted under a cabinet and handed it to Riley. "I did warn you that knife was sharp."

"Yes, you did." Riley sighed and wrapped the paper towel around his finger.

"Marlena!" David called from the bowels of the house. "Can you come and help me find the first aid kit?"

"It's under the bathroom counter!"

"Can't find it!"

"I'll be right there!" Marlena rolled her eyes. "Excuse me a minute. I swear it's right in front of him."

Once Marlena was gone, Hayden couldn't help herself. He looked so damned good. She walked closer, wondering if he smelled as good as he looked. Sure enough, he was wearing some yummy brand of aftershave. "Are you okay?"

"I'll live." His green eyes grew hot as he gazed at her. "But it's your fault."

"*My* fault? How can it be my fault?" Dear God, but she wanted to kiss him, which was so not appropriate. "I was clear across the room."

"And wearing a low-cut dress guaranteed to make a guy forget he's cutting radishes with a sharp knife." He glanced down at her cleavage before meeting her gaze again. "You did that on purpose, didn't you?"

"I have no idea what you're talking about." *Kiss me.*

"The hell you don't. One look at that neckline and I was transported back to a blanket in the bed of my pickup on a warm spring night with a very naked Hayden Manchester."

Heat curled between her legs, wound up through her belly, tightened her nipples, and finally flamed in her cheeks.

His eyes became as hot as molten glass. "I'm sure you planned it that way," he said softly.

"You're imagining things."

They'd come together as if magnetized, until the space

between them wasn't worth talking about. She knew from the way he was breathing that if she glanced at his fly, she'd probably see a bulge there. Tempting herself, she looked down. Sure enough.

"Happy, now, Hayden? You've had that effect on me ever since we hit puberty. Apparently nothing's changed in that department, either."

She looked into his eyes. "For you, maybe. I've moved on." *Liar.*

He swore under his breath. "If that's the way you feel, then why the hell did you wear that dress tonight?"

"Vanity," she admitted in a moment of brutal honesty. "I wanted to see if I could still turn you on."

"But nothing about me turns you on. Is that what you're saying?"

"Yes."

"Let's test that with a little kiss, shall we?"

Her heartbeat thundered in her ears. She glanced toward the ceiling. "I don't think that's allowed. There's no mistletoe."

"I don't need no stinkin' mistletoe." His arm went around her so fast that she barely had time to gasp in surprise before his mouth covered hers.

Ah, sweet heaven. No one kissed like Riley Kinnard. She'd told herself that time had enhanced her memory of his kiss, that nobody could measure up to the fantasy in her mind. It was no fantasy. He really performed this maneuver better than any man she'd ever been with, including one who was paid for doing it convincingly on camera.

Being in Riley's arms again, feeling the pressure of his lips and the thrust of his tongue was achingly familiar and so damned perfect that she wanted to weep. But she wouldn't. She'd give as good as she was getting.

Sliding her hands up his freshly shaven jaw, she tunneled her fingers through his dark hair as if they could pick up exactly where they'd left off. She cradled his head in both hands and deepened the kiss, wringing a moan from him that she hadn't heard in ten years. Once upon a time, that moan could very nearly make her climax. History seemed perfectly willing to repeat itself.

That wouldn't do. She couldn't allow Riley to kiss her into an orgasm in the middle of the Faulkners' kitchen. With deep regret, she pulled away from him and stepped back, her chest heaving.

He focused on her quivering breasts, then gazed at her lips, and finally looked into her eyes. His were filled with lust. She knew from past experience and late night confessions that he was imagining her naked, imagining them horizontal, imagining himself deep inside her.

Funny how ten years could fall away in an instant. She was stunned by how much power their attraction still held.

He seemed equally broadsided. Taking a deep breath, he cleared his throat. "Care to tell me again how unaffected you are, Hayden?"

"It doesn't matter if I'm affected or not."

"Because?"

"Because I'm taking a break from relationships for the time being."

He laughed. "No, you're not. A woman who's taking a break from relationships doesn't wear a dress like that."

"I shouldn't have worn it. It was a dumb impulse."

"Or a brilliant move that served to remind us both how much fun we used to have." He gazed at her. "You know, we could still—"

"Have fun again? Oh, I bet you'd love that, Riley." Anger replaced lust. He'd probably always thought of sex with her as an enjoyable pastime, while she'd thought of it as a lifetime commitment. They should have discussed their different views on what was happening between them their senior year, but they'd been too busy getting busy to do that. She'd made assumptions about his intentions that obviously hadn't been true.

"I think you'd love it, too, Hayden."

"Sorry, but the idea doesn't work for me." She'd had fun sex over in L.A. She wished that she could have fun sex with Riley, but now that she'd kissed him, she knew it would veer quickly from fun to significant, and that would be a huge mistake on her part.

"We have bandages!" Marlena's voice contained so much fake heartiness that no doubt the Faulkners had witnessed part or all of what had happened in the kitchen. Because they both seemed to be hoping for a rekindling of the flame, they'd probably waited to speak until they were sure the interlude was over.

Hayden wasn't particularly embarrassed to be caught kissing Riley. She'd known the Faulkners for so long that they were like family. But David would probably give her a hard time the next chance he had.

That chance came during dinner, when David offered to pour more wine. He walked around the table, refilling glasses. When he came to her chair, he held the bottle over her glass. "Are you *interested* in having more wine?" he asked, putting special emphasis on the word.

"Yes, thanks."

"David," Marlena said, "why are you talking weird?"

"Just a little joke between Hayden and me." He filled her glass to the top.

"Just because I'm interested in wine," Hayden said, "doesn't mean I'm interested in other stuff."

David snorted with laughter.

Riley gazed across the table at her. "Are you going to let us in on this joke?"

"No," Hayden said. "It's lame."

"I don't doubt it." Marlena passed the basket of beer bread. "David has a twisted sense of humor sometimes. Not to change the subject, but what do you guys think of this Damon Claus fellow? I'm happy for some help with the decorations, but there's a rogue element there. I hope he doesn't screw something up and burn down the house."

Riley spooned another helping of stew into his bowl. "I'll keep an eye on him. I've worked with enough subcontractors to be able to tell if he's competent or not. I can have him start on my parents' house first."

Hayden couldn't resist needling him on the subject. "What's up with that? I thought you were going to make do with the three spiral trees."

Riley looked disarmingly innocent. "When I saw how you were planning to surprise your folks, I decided to do the same for mine."

"BS, Kinnard. What about that we're number one sign you gave me from your front door? You're planning to turn this into a competition."

Riley gave her a lazy smile. "Maybe. Let me point out that you were quick to make the same gesture back at me."

"Reflex."

"Then I guess it's a good thing I didn't raise a different finger."

"You'd better watch out what you do with those fingers." Hayden eyed the bandaged ring finger on his left hand. Odd that he'd sliced that particular one, the one that remained bare, as did hers. "As proven tonight, you could hurt yourself."

"Kids, kids." David got up to pour more wine. "Make love, not war."

Riley glanced in Hayden's direction. "How about making love *and* war?"

Marlena frowned. "I don't think those go together."

"They might, if handled correctly." Riley held his glass for

David to top it off. "By the way, Hayden, speaking of competition, do you know what ever happened to that model of the *USS Arizona* we put together? And the blue ribbon we won?"

She hesitated to tell him they were still sitting in a glass cabinet in her parents' house. She could blame it on her parents being sentimental, but the truth was, she was worse about hanging on to stuff than they were. After all, they'd been willing to sell the house, and she hadn't wanted it to leave the family.

Finally she came up with a response for Riley. "Why, do you want them back?"

"Maybe."

Her tummy churned. She didn't want to give them to him. What if he lost them? Could she pretend she didn't know where they were? Probably not. She was horrible at lying.

"I remember that model," David said.

"Me, too." Marlena buttered her bread. "We took a trip out to the fairgrounds specifically to see it. Do you still have it, Hayden?"

She could stall with Riley, but not Marlena, who had been a good friend to her over the years. "Yes, I do. It's in a cabinet in the house, along with the ribbon. My folks kept them, and I've…" She didn't want to admit how much they meant to her, because Riley might misinterpret that as her still being hung up on him. "I've been trying to decide what to do with them."

"Give them to me, then," Riley said. "I'll save them for my kids."

That stung. Hayden remembered a time when she'd thought she'd be the mother of his kids. "What about my kids? They might be interested."

"There's that word again—interested," David said.

"Tell you what." Hayden wasn't about to make a decision about the model and ribbon after two and a half glasses of wine. "Assuming you move back to Tucson, we'll work something out. I mean, we're talking about our kids…I mean, the kids we each have separately. With different people." She couldn't seem to discuss this without sounding like an idiot. "Anyway, neither one of us is even married, let alone pregnant."

Marlena laughed. "If Riley gets pregnant, we're calling the *Enquirer*. Which reminds me, Hayden. What's the latest gossip about Britney Spears?"

Hayden was more than happy to move the conversation away from the model she and Riley had built together and potential kids that they weren't going to have together. Celebrity gossip took up the rest of the evening, lasting all the way through cheesecake and the best coffee Hayden had ever tasted.

Dessert was served in the living room so everyone could enjoy the Christmas tree. It was decorated, as always, with ornaments from all over the world, plus some homemade ones, including two that Hayden had created in grade school.

"The tree smells great," Riley set down his empty coffee mug. "I was kind of sad to find out my folks put up an artificial one."

"They told me," Hayden said. "They figured you wouldn't be happy about it, but they like the convenience."

"Maybe when I'm back in town permanently, I can convince them to go back to a real tree if I help them with it."

Hayden took a last swallow of her coffee. "I offered to do that, but they wouldn't let me."

"Yeah, but I'm their kid."

"I'm practically their kid. They let me help them paint the guest room as if I were one of the family. I think they're just done with all the work of Christmas."

Marlena sighed. "I suppose it can happen. Fortunately, I still love everything connected with the holidays. Well, except having David slice himself to ribbons putting lights on the cactus. I'm glad Damon Claus will do that this year." She picked up the coffee carafe. "Who's ready for a refill?"

"No more for me, thanks." Hayden picked up her mug and dessert plate. "This has been fabulous, though." She turned to Marlena, who had joined her on the couch. "Let me give you a hand with the dishes." By rights she and Riley should be doing the dishes, but that would put them alone in the kitchen again.

Marlena shook her head. "I appreciate the offer, but David and I have a routine. We're far more efficient if we're left to do it ourselves. Riley can walk you home."

Hayden recognized a bad idea when she heard one. "That's silly. I'm only going across the street."

Riley had been occupying one of the easychairs, and now he stood. "My mother would have my ass if I didn't walk a lady home after dinner. You wouldn't want me to get in trouble with my mom, would you?"

"You won't get in trouble unless you tell her," Hayden said.

David had quietly left the room and now came back with Hayden's wool coat and Riley's leather jacket. "If he doesn't tell her, I will. She asked me to keep an eye on him, and I take that job seriously."

Hayden realized she was dealing with a Faulkner conspiracy. Obviously, the search for the first aid kit earlier had been a ploy to leave Riley and her alone, as well. She couldn't get out of having Riley walk her to her door without sounding ungracious, so she'd go along with that. But she was on her guard and wasn't about to participate in any good-night kisses, let alone what might logically follow a good-night kiss or two, or six.

She managed to put on her own coat quickly enough that Riley had no chance to help her with it. Her vulnerability to his touch could get her into a whole lot of trouble, so she'd keep her distance.

Both she and Riley heaped praise on the dinner and the company before heading out the door, each of them laden with Tupperware containers of beef stew, beer bread and cheesecake. Hayden smiled. The Faulkners hadn't stopped to think that holding leftovers would take the romance right out of a good-night moment at her front door. They'd unwittingly sabotaged their own matchmaking efforts by making sure that both Hayden and Riley had their hands full.

"Nothing against my mom's cooking," Riley said as he followed Hayden down the flagstone walkway, "but I've never tasted anything better than that meal in my life."

"Me, either." Hayden stepped carefully to avoid taking a nosedive by catching her heel in an uneven part of the flagstone. "If those two ever get tired of teaching, they could open a restaurant."

"I asked them about that once, and they said cooking for pay would put too much pressure on them. They'd rather give away what they make to friends and family."

"Lucky us, to be counted as friends." There was no traffic, so she started across the street.

"That's for sure." Riley fell into step beside her. Then he glanced up at the sky. "Nice night for stars."

"Uh-huh." She hoped he wasn't planning to make another reference to the many nights they'd shared under a similar sky. If so, she'd shut him down immediately.

"That was something else about Chicago. You can't see the stars from the downtown area. Too many lights."

So he hadn't been trying to work around to the subject of sex. Good thing he hadn't, because she was not going there. She followed his conversational lead. "I got sick of the L.A. traffic, all the people, the constant frenzy. Mostly, though, I just missed being home. I didn't think I would."

"I know. Neither did I. When you're eighteen, all you can think about is going somewhere else."

"Somewhere more exciting."

"Right. Although I can't deny that Chicago was exciting."

"I'll bet." As she led him up her walkway, she vowed not to think of the girls he'd slept with in Chicago. It was none of her business. "L.A. was exciting, too."

"I'm sure."

Instead of a front porch, her house had a small patio surrounded by a low stucco wall and a wrought iron gate. Hayden was afraid if she tried to open the gate while holding her leftovers, she'd drop something precious, like her slice of cheesecake. She turned to Riley. "Would you mind holding these things while I get myself through the gate and take out my key?"

"Nope. Load me up."

Something about hearing his voice in this very spot triggered memories of all the times he'd walked her to her door when they'd been dating, and all the passionate kisses they'd shared standing on this small patio. Sure as torrential rains hit during a desert monsoon season, she was turned on again.

She couldn't give him the Tupperware without touching him briefly, so she pretended he was somebody she didn't like. There was a slimy producer who had tried to get her into bed, and if she narrowed her eyes, she could almost imagine Riley was him.

Almost, but not quite. She still had the urge to jump Riley's bones, but if she hurried, she could be through the gate and inside her house before her hormones took over.

"Are you going to a fire or something?"

"No." She practically ran to her front door. "I'm just getting cold."

"In that case, how about—"

"Don't say it." Opening the door with a flourish, she grabbed her containers out of his arms. "Thanks and good night."

"Hey, I think you took both slices of cheesecake!"

"I don't think so. Bye." She closed the door with her hip

and leaned against it, panting. That was close. As she walked back to the kitchen to put away the leftovers, she became aware that her panties were actually damp. That man had way too much sex appeal. She needed to avoid him as much as possible.

Shoving the containers into the refrigerator, she noticed that she had four, not three. She had snagged his cheesecake, after all. Oh, well. She could deal with it tomorrow. Daylight should make it easier to do. She wouldn't be so vulnerable to her memories of being naked with Riley.

He'd looked good naked at eighteen. She wondered if he looked better naked at twenty-eight. Probably. Men tended to bulk up a little more in their twenties. But she wouldn't be finding out how he looked naked.

Her doorbell rang.

Crossing the darkened living room, she put her eye to the peephole. Riley stood there, minus his Tupperware. She didn't think she was strong enough to face him a second time.

But not answering the bell would be rude, especially because she knew what he was after. She opened the door. "Yes, I took your cheesecake by mistake. I'll go get it."

"That isn't why I'm here."

*Oh, dear God.* She turned and discovered he'd come inside. She didn't want him inside. They were way too alone inside. Maybe she should keep pretending it was all about the cheesecake. "Stay right there. I'll bring it to you."

"Hayden, what's wrong? You're acting as if you're afraid of me." He walked into the kitchen looking like all her hormone-drenched fantasies come true.

"I'm not afraid of you. It's me I'm afraid of." She took out the cheesecake container, slammed the refrigerator door, and handed him the Tupperware. She wanted him so much she was shaking.

"Self-loathing is bad for you. I learned that in psychology class."

"I know." She combed her hair away from her face. "I'll walk you to the door."

"Look, what I really came for was—"

"I know. God, I *know*." She gave up. He was too yummy. She ripped the Tupperware out of his hand, set it on the counter, and flung herself into his arms. "I've changed my mind, Kinnard. Let's do each other and get it over with."

# 3

THE PAYOFF for locking himself out had never been this huge. He wasn't about to tell her he'd come back for the spare key, not when she was kissing him with the kind of energy that could light up a good-size city. Finally, *finally* he could do what he'd been dying to do all night. He reached for the back zipper of her dress.

She squirmed away from him. "Not here." Grabbing his hand, she tugged him out of the kitchen and through the darkened living room filled with the scent of a live Christmas tree.

He didn't comment on that, either. He didn't intend to open his mouth, except to kiss her until her eyes rolled back in her head. Contemplating what lay ahead of him, he could barely walk. He hoped she wasn't taking him far.

She wasn't. She pulled him into the promising shadows of the master bedroom where he made out the vague outline of a bed. About that time he remembered that he hadn't anticipated this event and he hadn't made any preparations. He'd always been responsible for condoms in the past.

So he'd have to risk saying something, and he'd better say it soon, because she'd helped him out of his jacket and was unbuttoning his shirt. Her lips had found his again, and any second his brain would short circuit and his buddy inside his Jockeys would be in charge.

It took a concerted effort to abandon the delicious pleasures of her mouth so he could talk. But he did it for the good of the order. "Hayden, I don't have anything. I didn't bring—"

Breathing hard, she backed away from him. "Why the hell not?"

He squeezed his eyes shut. If he'd come over here to have sex, he should have brought a condom. Now that he'd admitted to not having one, he had two choices. He could either tell her his real reason for being here or look like an idiot who'd forgotten to bring the freaking birth control.

It was no contest. "I forgot."

"Riley! That's terrible! How could you forget something like that?"

"I don't know." And for the rest of the week, he'd be packin'. For now though, he had to improvise. He moved in again and took her in his arms. "We'll work around it."

"But—"

He silenced her protest with a kiss he hoped would remind her that they did have other options. They'd learned a lot about sex the spring of their senior year, and he knew how to give her a good time even without a little raincoat. She knew how to give him one, too, if she wasn't too ticked off about the condom.

She was somewhat ticked off. He could tell by the way she held back from kissing him fully. But moments later, she'd surrendered, melting against him in that familiar way that drove him crazy. He loved her body, loved the way it fit so perfectly against his, as if they'd been designed specifically for each other. He hadn't realized how special that was ten years ago, but he was more knowledgeable now.

He wished they had every possibility open to them tonight, but considering that he hadn't expected anything at all, he'd count his blessings and enjoy what he could. Undressing her was another skill he'd perfected. He was gratified to discover she still preferred bras that fastened in the back. The front-hook ones were supposed to be easier to maneuver, but he'd done all his practicing on Hayden's, and back closures were the kind he liked.

Once her bra was tossed to the floor, he took his reward in both hands. Ah. *This* was how a woman's breasts were supposed to feel. He kneaded them gently, touching her the way he knew she liked to be touched, brushing his thumbs over her nipples until she trembled. The room was dark, but he didn't need any light to know exactly how she looked right now, her skin rosy from his caress, her nipples puckered with excitement.

She would be wet by now. Sliding his hand under the elastic of her panties, he confirmed that fact as he continued to plunder her mouth with his tongue. Her moan was his cue to pay attention to her sweet little clit and slide his fingers in where his penis wouldn't get to go tonight. He promised himself to make up for that mistake soon.

For now, he'd tend to her needs. And although he hadn't had his hand inside her panties in ten years, he hadn't forgotten a single move. They'd danced this dance so many times that he knew the exact rhythm and pressure guaranteed to rock her world.

Like that. There. Almost. And…*now.* She wrenched her mouth from his and gasped as the convulsions shook her. Hooking his arm around her waist, he held her upright as her knees threatened to buckle. He pressed the pads of his fingers against the quivering wall of her vagina, knowing that gave her a deeper orgasm.

A rush of possessiveness took him by surprise. He didn't want to think about anyone else doing this during the time they'd been apart, but he couldn't help himself. He hated that she'd had other lovers, and hated caring about it even more. After all, he'd had other lovers, too.

Except he knew they hadn't compared to Hayden. He wanted to know the same thing was true for her, but he couldn't very well ask if she'd had better sex with someone else. That would sound pathetic and needy.

So he'd do the next best thing. He'd ramped up the action. Easing his fingers from action central, he scooped her up and carried her the short distance to the bed. Now that his eyes had adjusted, he could see the room more clearly. The bed was covered with a dark-patterned quilt.

Other than noticing the quilt, he was too busy making sure he didn't drop her to observe anything else. He used to be able to carry her with ease in his football days. She wasn't any heavier now, which told him he'd better take up weight-training again soon. Whatever the reason, he was grateful the bed was only steps away.

She moaned softly as he laid her across the mattress with her knees at the edge and her legs dangling. "Thank you," she murmured.

"For getting you to the bed without dropping you?"

She was still breathing hard. "For getting me to the finish line in less than sixty seconds."

"You were timing me?"

"No, but you were…very fast."

He peeled her panties down and tossed them on the floor, too. "The next time will take a little longer." He dropped to his knees beside the bed.

She levered herself up onto her elbows. "But it's your turn, now."

"We're skipping my turn." But he was heartened to know she had thought of him.

"I don't think that's fair."

"Stop thinking." He parted her thighs and settled in to prove that he had the most talented tongue in the West.

RILEY NEEDN'T HAVE BOTHERED with the command. Once Hayden felt his hot breath against her slick thighs, all thoughts disappeared. Ten years ago, he'd been great at this, but now… Now he was systematically turning her into a writhing, panting, shameless wild woman.

She cradled his head and ran trembling fingers around the inside of his ears as she gloried in the sensations washing over her. She propped her heels on the mattress and wiggled closer, not wanting to miss a single swipe of his tongue. Her grip on his head tightened. Oh…sweet…heaven.

Her world pulsed in time to the movement of his mouth. Erotic, liquid sounds blended with her urgent whimpers as he coaxed her back to the brink. She wasn't so quick to get there this time. The tiny part of her brain that still worked rejoiced in that.

Taking longer to climax meant she could revel in his artistry and savor the flush of desire rolling through her, receding, then rolling through again. The waves flashed in color through her mind, starting out pink, shading toward fuschia, then moving into deep orange that gradually trans-formed into a rich, velvet red.

She was on fire for him, the flames of her waiting orgasm licking at her self control with every rapid movement of his tongue. At last she couldn't hold back the flood another second. She let go, let go with a cry of triumph and pleasure, the sort of wanton celebration she'd never allowed herself before, not even with him.

He planted wet kisses all the way back up her naked body until he reached her mouth, which he claimed with confi-dence. As well he should. He'd turned her inside out. As her sluggish brain struggled toward a coherent thought, only one surfaced. She was so screwed.

She hadn't wanted to give him the upper hand, but she'd done exactly that. He was the victor in this round unless… unless she turned the tables on him and gave him an even better orgasm.

She didn't know if that was humanly possible, but it was worth a try. His unsteady breathing and the urgent press of his penis through the fabric of his slacks told her he was more than ready for whatever she decided to dish out. Maybe she could reclaim some of the territory she'd lost.

Cupping his face in both hands, she lifted his mouth away from hers. "Your turn," she murmured.

He leaned down and brushed a soft kiss over her lips. "Not tonight." Then he pushed himself away from the bed.

*What?* She'd never known Riley to turn down a blow job. "No fair!"

His answering chuckle was soft and intimate. "All's fair in love and war." He walked out of the bedroom.

She sat up, ready to run after him and demand an explanation. But she was naked, and running after him sent the wrong message, anyway. Moments later, she heard the front door open and close.

Damn that man! He'd deliberately left things unbalanced between them, so that he could prove…what? That she needed sex more than he did?

Well, she didn't. He'd regret the moment he turned her down, by God. It'd be a cold day in hell before she made that offer, or any other, again to the infuriating Riley Kinnard.

Climbing out of bed, she stalked to the closet, pulled on a robe, and went in search of a pad of paper. Her plans for her front yard display had just grown a whole lot bigger.

RILEY'S INTERVIEW the next morning went reasonably well, considering he'd had very little sleep the night before. A hand-job in the shower hadn't kept him from lying awake most of the night, wanting like hell to go back across the street with a supply of condoms. But he was proud of himself for resisting.

He drove from the interview back to his parents' house, behind the wheel of his parents' Lincoln—so not his style.

On the way, he prepared himself to find Hayden working in the yard. He would play it cool, no matter how much the sight of her made him hot.

He hadn't intended to get into a battle with her. Or maybe he had. That's the way he and Hayden rolled—either sparring or making love. He'd never found a woman who was so infuriating and exciting in equal measures.

She'd definitely fired the first shot in the area of sex by showing up at the Faulkners in that do-me-now dress. Then she'd shut him down, only to throw herself at him later on.

Those kind of mixed signals meant he needed to keep his wits about him if he didn't want to end up as a smear on the bottom of her shoe as she tromped him into the dirt. She could do it, too. Ten years ago she'd dumped him over one tiny infraction. He'd told her Lisa had set him up, but that hadn't cut any ice with Hayden.

She'd thrown it all away because of one silly kiss, one grope that Lisa had staged entirely for Hayden's benefit. Riley had been thinking about marriage, although he'd known both he and Hayden would have to finish college first. Still, he'd seriously considered getting engaged. Then everything had blown up.

Last night had reminded him how much he loved loving Hayden, so he had to be careful. Leaving when he was ahead had been a brilliant move. Extremely difficult to do, but brilliant.

Thinking of Hayden was giving him a hard-on, so he forced himself to concentrate on his job prospects. His next interview was critical. It was for the only company he was interested in, mostly because they were so careful about the architects they hired. The interview process would take up his mornings all week, and he liked that kind of thoroughness.

He hoped he'd get the job, because despite his decent situation in Chicago, he was ready to come home. He wanted to see more of his folks and raise his kids here, assuming he had some.

Hayden wouldn't be a part of that, he kept telling himself. He'd be better off starting fresh with someone else, someone without all the history, someone who wasn't holding a grudge against him. Yet for this week, he'd take whatever came his way, Hayden-wise, so long as he could maintain some kind of control and not get his heart handed to him on a plate…again.

He also planned to kick butt when it came to the front yard Christmas display. My God, he was an architect. That should count for something. Because his afternoon was free, he'd asked Damon to come by after lunch with the materials so they could get started.

Damon's truck, a black monster with enough shiny chrome to induce snow blindness, was already parked in front of Riley's house. The truck bed was stacked with plywood and two-by-fours. Damon wasn't in the truck, though. He was over in Hayden's yard, talking to her while she worked with a post-hole digger.

Riley couldn't blame Damon for wandering over there. Today Hayden wore Daisy Dukes and a red halter top. Sure, it was warm, close to eighty, but that outfit wasn't about the weather.

Hayden had worn that outfit on purpose, just as she'd worn the dress on purpose. She wanted him to want her, but her motives were suspect. This afternoon she could be trying to teach Riley a lesson for walking out on her last night. She could be reeling him in so she could slam dunk him later on.

Whatever her plan, it was working. He regretted the stupid impulse that had made him leave. Staying in control of the situation had seemed so important a few minutes ago, before he'd laid eyes on Hayden in those short shorts and halter top.

Good thing traffic was light on this street, because Riley realized he'd been sitting in the middle of the street with the engine idling while he gawked at Hayden. Neither she nor

Claus had turned in his direction. Riley wanted to break up that little conversation. Claus was the kind of guy who'd push his luck if he thought he had a shot.

Pulling past his driveway and coming alongside Claus's truck, Riley slid down the Lincoln's window. "Hey, Damon! You about ready to get started over here?"

Claus turned around and waved. "Sure thing! Just checking out the competition."

Leaning on her post-hole digger, Hayden glanced over her shoulder, as if she'd had no idea he'd been there all along. "Hi, Riley!" She flashed him a big smile before going back to her digging. *Backside in motion.* During his football days, they'd had a joke about that.

At the moment it was no joke. He wondered how he could get rid of Claus so he could go over to Hayden's house and suggest they share a pitcher of lemonade in the backyard. He remembered that backyard—an oasis that would be perfect for some outdoor sex.

As he considered the possibilities, he became so mesmerized by the wiggle of her denim-clad rear that he took his foot off the brake and the Lincoln rolled forward. He almost hit Claus, who was crossing in front of him to get back to his truck.

Claus leaped back, obviously startled. Riley slammed on the brakes and brought the Lincoln to a halt. *Damnation.*

"Sorry!" he yelled out the window.

Hayden turned. "Were you talking to me?"

"No," he called out. "To Claus."

"Figures."

"Yeah." Claus seemed to have recovered himself. He gave Riley an evil grin before turning back to Hayden. "He almost hit me because he was so busy watching you dig that hole."

And speaking of digging holes, Claus was helping him dig a huge one for himself. The guy was becoming a royal pain in the ass.

"Were you ogling me, Riley?" Hayden smiled again, and this time that smile was filled with self-satisfaction. "I thought you were immune."

"I was trying to figure out what you're building, that's all." She'd probably know he was lying, but it was worth a try.

"A corral."

"Oh. I see." He didn't, really. A corral seemed like unnecessary work unless…then he remembered the live animals in the Manchesters' manger scene ten years ago. "You wouldn't be thinking of bringing real horses in, would you?"

She gazed at him with a smug expression.

"Duly noted."

"Happy decorating!" She turned back to her post-hole digging.

So she was bringing in live animals. That meant he'd have to think of something equally spectacular, like moving parts on his cityscape. She was challenging him, and she'd always admired a guy who would meet her challenge. If he wanted to get her naked again, he'd have to have her believing he would put up one hell of a Christmas display.

He *would* put up one hell of a Christmas display. He wasn't sure of her motivation, but he was becoming clear about his. Ten years ago she'd kicked him to the curb. He wanted to prove she'd made a mistake in doing that.

## 4

BECAUSE SHE WASN'T setting the posts in cement, Hayden finished the corral before dark and went inside to shower and change. She was curious about what Riley and Damon were building over in the garage across the street. So far nothing had gone up on the lawn except some two-by-four supports, which suggested a rather large structure was coming. She could smell paint fumes wafting from the garage, too.

Earlier in the day, Damon had tried to find out what her plans were, because he could tell she was adding features to the bunkhouse display. She hadn't told him, although Riley had guessed about the live horses. Little did Riley know that was only the beginning.

She'd had a shower and was toweling dry when the phone rang. Wrapping the towel around her, she walked into the bedroom and glanced at the caller ID display. Riley. A stronger woman would have let him leave a message.

Hayden was strong, but not that strong. From the moment the phone had first rung, her pulse rate had spiked. She'd had a hunch it was Riley. She hoped he was still thinking about her Daisy Dukes.

Steadying her breathing, she picked up the phone. "Hey, Riley."

"You still have my cheesecake."

She'd thought about the extra cheesecake several times

during the day and had decided to wait and see if he used it as an excuse to call. "Maybe I ate it."

"Both pieces?"

"Could be. I put in a long day."

"In minimal clothing. You fight dirty."

Hayden smiled. "You're the one who said all's fair in love and war."

"And you'll be sorry tomorrow afternoon when I go shirtless in my yard."

"I'll bet you don't have the muscles you used to have, Kinnard."

"How do you know I don't?"

"Because you almost dropped me carrying me over to the bed." She wondered if this conversation was having the same effect on him that it was on her.

Could be, because his voice sounded a trifle husky when he asked his next question. "Did you really eat all the cheesecake?"

"No." She lowered her voice to a sexy purr. "Want to come get it?"

"You're killing me, Manchester."

Aha! A chink in his armor. "Not enough, apparently. You were able to leave last night."

"You don't know how hard it was."

This time she couldn't control her laughter. "Oh, yes, I do. You kept shoving it against my thigh."

He groaned. "I should know better than to get into a verbal sparring match with you. Look, this proposition has all the romantic flavor of a night at Chuck E Cheese's, but what do you say we share leftovers at my house?"

"I have a feeling there's more to the invitation than meets the eye." Under the towel, her nipples tightened and dampness seeped between her thighs as she considered what that more might be.

"You might want to wear sexy underwear."

With this kind of phone foreplay, they wouldn't get to the food for hours. "Or no underwear at all."

He drew in a quick breath. "How soon can you come?"

"Any minute now."

"I meant come over here. God, you're incorrigible."

"All's fair in—"

"Yeah, yeah, yeah. I'll leave the door unlocked."

"Where will you be?"

"Use your imagination, Manchester. I'm sure you'll be able to find me."

Just like that, they'd set up a sexual meeting. And she could hardly wait. Tossing the towel aside, she dabbed on a little perfume, but she was too impatient to mess with makeup. She ran a brush through her damp hair and called it good.

Taking a pair of soft gray sweatpants out of the drawer, she pulled them on and felt the sensual buzz of the material everywhere it touched. The sweatshirt she grabbed was yellow, but it could have been any color for all she cared. This was expediency, not a fashion statement.

She shoved her feet into loafers, grabbed her keys from a hook by the door, and was partway down the walk before she remembered the leftovers. Grumbling, she went back for the containers as the phone started ringing again.

Laughing, she grabbed the receiver in the kitchen, certain it was Riley wanting to know why she wasn't across the street and in his bed yet. "You need to put a leash on those hormones, Kinnard," she said.

"Hayden?" Her mother sounded confused. "Which one of the Kinnards are you referring to?"

Hayden gulped. It was one thing to allow herself to be seduced by an old flame. It was something else to have to explain that to the woman who'd held her while she'd sobbed out her anguish over that very same old flame. At the time,

Hayden had vowed to die before she ever gave Riley so much as the time of day.

"Um, Riley's home for the week. He's interviewing for a job at a few architectural firms here."

Her mother's tone was cautious. No doubt she was wondering if she dared ask about Hayden's first comment. "That'll be nice for his parents. I'm sure they're glad to have him back."

Hayden could simply agree with that statement, but her parents would be here in three weeks, and they would certainly spend time with the Kinnards. The cruise would be discussed, no question. "They're not here this week. They went on a cruise they won in some contest."

"Oh." Hayden's mother hesitated. "So you thought I was Riley calling, didn't you?"

"Well, I—"

"Listen, you've lived on your own for a long time in L.A. and I don't want to imply that you don't know what you're doing."

"I'll be fine, Mom." Wow, how awkward was this? Her mother could easily guess that sex was on the agenda tonight. Why else would she refer to putting hormones on a leash?

"It's only that I remember how devastated you were in high school when he got involved with that other girl. Maybe it's because we're so far away up here in Washington, but… you're usually so self-sufficient, and he's the one man who seems to have the power to hurt you. I would hate to see him break your heart a second time."

"That makes two of us."

"So be careful, Hayden."

"I will, Mom. Thanks. Was there a reason you called?"

"Oh! I nearly forgot. Your dad mentioned that it would be sort of sad to come back for Christmas and have no decorations in the front yard. Would you be willing to put up a little something? Maybe one of those blow-up Santas or the deer family that lights up. Just something."

"Sure. Be happy to."

"Don't go to a lot of trouble."

"Believe me, it's no trouble." Her trouble was on the other side of the street.

"So, how's everything? How soon do you have to go on location for your next film?"

"The middle of January." Hayden was not in the mood for a chat. She had to get off the phone and decide what to do about Riley. Her mother was right—having sex with him was dangerous. But could she resist?

"I thought while we were back in town, we could take a few side trips, maybe go down to Bisbee and Tombstone. Would you like that?"

"Sounds great." How could she get off the phone and not sound as if she could hardly wait to run across the street for wild monkey sex?

"Oh, and you and I need to have lunch at Tohono Chul. I love their tearoom."

Hayden's eyes crossed. She suspected her mother of deliberately keeping her on the line to protect her honor. "I'd love that, Mom. Listen, I—"

Her doorbell rang.

"Someone's at the door." She had a pretty good idea who it was.

"Go ahead and answer it. I'll wait."

*No, don't wait!* But it was her mother, and her mother had radar when it came to these things. "Be right back." She wasn't the least surprised to open the door and find Riley, also dressed in sweats and a sweatshirt. He carried a small shopping bag.

"You were taking forever, so I decided to bring the party over here," he said. "I mean, one bed's as good as—"

She clamped a hand over his mouth and jerked a thumb back toward the kitchen. "My mother's on the phone," she murmured.

"Oh." He lowered his voice. "She pretty much hates me, right?"

"Pretty much. And when I picked up the phone, I thought it was you, so I said something fairly incriminating."

"She knows we're about to do the nasty?"

"'Fraid so."

"*Awk*ward."

"No kidding. I should go back and tell her…tell her…"

"Tell her that what happened with Lisa Trenton was all a misunderstanding."

Hayden frowned at him. "Yeah, right."

"I swear it was, Hayden. I tried to explain, but you wouldn't listen."

"Translation—you tried to make excuses for playing tonsil hockey with another girl and feeling her up. How could you after all those nights we spent together? Was I your learner girl, the one you used to try out those positions in *The Joy of Sex* so you could act worldly with the likes of Lisa?"

"Uh, Hayden, you're getting loud. Your mother might be able to hear you."

"Well, that's no problem, because I know what I'm going to tell her." Hayden stomped back to the kitchen. "Mom, that was Riley, but don't worry. I'm sending him back across the street."

"That's good, Hayden. I don't trust that boy."

*He's a man, now, Mom. And I want him more than ever.* "I don't trust him, either," she said. "Anyway, I'd better get off the phone so I can take care of that."

"Call me back if you need to talk, sweetie."

"I will. Thanks. Give my love to Dad." She hung up the phone and turned to discover that Riley had come into the kitchen and was now inches away. "You need to leave," she said, not daring to look into his eyes. "This is a really bad idea. So go."

"Ten years ago I obeyed that command. Now I have the balls to challenge it." He pulled her into his arms and lifted her chin. "Tell me you don't want this." Then he kissed her.

She put up a token resistance, and then she caved. *Sorry, Mom. He's here and you're not. I'll give him up tomorrow.*

RILEY WAS PUSHING his luck, and he knew it. Even after all this time, Hayden was ready to crucify him over the Lisa Trenton episode. So was Mrs. Manchester, apparently. He could end up being rejected all over again.

But Hayden's kiss didn't taste like rejection. It tasted like surrender. Judging by the way she felt as she plastered her luscious body against his, she'd had big plans before that phone call, big plans that didn't include underwear. Holding her was like holding a woman wearing pajamas. He'd never seduced Hayden while she was in pajamas, but it would probably feel a lot like this.

Fortunately he was wearing the equivalent of pajamas, too. Twenty minutes ago he'd been naked, but impatience had spurred him to pull on sweats and a sweatshirt, stuff his bare feet into running shoes, and cross the street. Good thing he had.

Another few minutes on the phone with her mother and Hayden would've cancelled the show. He'd arrived in the nick of time.

He had his hands under her shirt by the time she started backing them out of the kitchen. He figured she was heading toward the bedroom, but they never got that far. He'd always wanted to make love to her beside a fragrant Christmas tree, and now was as good a time as any.

He framed her face in both hands and drew back from her potent kiss. "Here."

Her words were slurred with passion. "On the floor?"

"Yeah. By the tree."

"Okay." She kicked off her loafers.

Getting them both down onto the Berber rug took some management on his part, and he wasn't able to completely remove their clothes. He did, however, fish the condom out of his pocket before shoving the sweats to his ankles and kneeling between her spread thighs.

The light from the kitchen gave him the required visibility for rolling on the condom, although with this kind of motivation, he could have done it in complete darkness.

She was breathing hard, but she managed to get in a dig. "I see you remembered this time."

"I'm a quick study."

"Then you must know how much I want you to do me, Kinnard."

"I think so. You agreed to the floor."

"Couldn't be any worse than the bed of your truck."

He was stung. "I put a piece of foam under the blanket!"

"One inch."

"I was saving your reputation! If I'd bought it any thicker, everyone would have known what I wanted it for!"

She caressed his bare chest. "They knew, anyway. Are we doing this or not?"

"We are." He reached between her thighs and groaned at how wet she was. "We sure as hell are." The moment he slid into her, he realized that he'd made a mistake. It felt too good.

She might be allowing this now, but there was no guarantee she'd allow it in the future. He was suddenly all about the future, and he wanted her in it.

She sucked in a breath.

"Is anything wrong?" He was ready to rock and roll, but maybe she wasn't as ready as she felt.

"No." She said it as if she had something clogging her throat.

"I haven't been here for a while." *And it's great, absolutely great.* "I don't want to hurt you."

"You're not hurting me, okay?"

He leaned close and brushed his lips over hers. "I never wanted to hurt you, Hayden."

"So you say." Her voice sounded funny.

"You're not going to cry or anything, are you?"

"Definitely not." She sniffed. "It's just that…I've missed you."

That sounded promising. "I've missed you, too, Hayden. Don't cry, sweetheart."

"It's allergies." She sniffed again. "Could you just get on with this, please?"

"Absolutely." But she was crying. He kissed her eyes, her cheeks, her mouth, and they all tasted of tears. "Hayden…"

"Never mind! Get busy!"

So he did, thinking if he gave her an orgasm, she might forget to cry. It didn't quite work out that way. The closer she was to coming, the faster her tears fell. Knowing Hayden, she'd hate that she was so emotional about their sexual reunion, but he didn't hate it. He loved knowing she still cared that much.

He'd show her he still cared, too, by making sure he did this the way she'd always liked it done. When she lifted her hips, he angled his to make sure he caught her G-spot. They'd learned about that all-important G-spot together, and he knew right where hers lived.

"Oh, Riley." She dug her fingers into the muscles of his backside and met him thrust for thrust.

"Yeah, Hayden. Go for it, girl." She might be crying, but she was as intent on her climax as he was. He'd learned ten years ago that if she had an orgasm, his would follow with no prompting. So hers was the first order of business.

And they were almost there. His heart raced in anticipation. He'd forgotten what a thrill ride sex could be with Hayden. She gave it all she had. But damn, she was still crying, and her crying was getting louder.

He barely had enough breath to ask the question, but she worried him. "Are you okay?"

"I'm ducky!" She gasped and picked up the pace. "Just keep...doing...*that*. Right there. More. Yes! *Yes!*" With a sob, she lifted into orbit.

He followed her into the stratosphere, and his climax launched him like the afterburners on a rocket. Only Hayden could produce that sensation in him. *Only Hayden.*

# 5

"SO WHAT ARE WE DOING on the floor?" Hayden nudged Riley, who lay like a dead person on top of her. "Whose bright idea was this?" She'd let the emotion drain out of her before rousing him. Now she had her 'tude on again. It was bad enough that she'd turned into a water faucet while they were having sex without having to talk about it afterward.

With a sigh, Riley pushed himself up on his elbows and gazed down at her. "It was my idea. I love Christmas. I love Christmas trees. I knew I'd love doing it with you beside the tree."

Oh, damn. All that love talk, even if it wasn't directed specifically at her, was making the lump come back into her throat. Her eyes had started leaking again, too.

Riley peered at her. "Are you crying again?"

"No." She pushed at his chest. "It's your aftershave. It's making my eyes water."

"You are a lousy liar, Hayden."

"I'm not lying." She tried to wiggle out from under him.

"Stop that or you'll dislodge something critical."

She went completely still. They'd been extremely careful about birth control ten years ago. No reason to be careless now. "Then let me up."

"Not until we talk about this crying thing. If there's a problem, maybe I can fix it."

Fat chance of that, unless he had a time machine. In the

dim light filtering in from the kitchen, she couldn't tell that he was ten years older. This could be the Christmas of their senior year. She'd had such faith in him then.

But she didn't really want to go back, didn't want to give up all that she'd learned and accomplished since high school. If only Riley could do that superhero trick—spin the world backward, rethink his decision to kiss Lisa and put his hand on her boob, and then fast forward to the present.

She'd learned a hard lesson when she'd caught him with Lisa. Riley hadn't been as into their relationship as she'd been. If he had been, he would have apologized for what happened instead of making excuses and trying to exonerate himself of any blame.

"Talk to me, Hayden."

"It's too late to fix it," she said.

"It's never too late unless you're dead."

"If you don't let me up, you're gonna be dead, Riley, and then it will really be too late. Don't try those strong-arm tactics on me. I don't like it."

He stared down at her, as if trying to look into her eyes. "Okay. I'll let you up, but I want you to promise me that we'll talk about this crying business."

"Now there's a pointless conversation." Since he couldn't change the past, she had no interest in talking about it. "It is what it is. Or it is what it was. Whatever."

"Promise me we'll talk over dinner."

She sighed. "You can talk over dinner. How's that?"

"Good enough." He eased away from her.

She was thankful for the darkness, because this was always the awkward part of sex. Condoms were never going to be a graceful solution, no matter how many ribs they had or how colorful they were. She longed for a committed relationship where she and the guy could work out alternatives to latex. But she couldn't commit to someone until she found someone who measured up to Riley. And Riley couldn't be trusted. What a mess.

Scrambling back into her sweatpants and sweatshirt, she combed her fingers through her hair and walked unsteadily back into the kitchen. Riley packed quite a sexual punch—he always had. Maybe he'd ruined her for anyone else, in more ways than one.

By the time he walked into the kitchen, she had their stew warming in a saucepan on the stove, and the beer bread in the toaster oven. "There's wine in the rack over there." She pointed out the one she'd bought after moving in. "And a corkscrew in the drawer right below the rack."

Riley seemed perfectly at home opening the wine and searching the cupboards until he found the wine glasses. He should feel at home, Hayden thought. He'd been in this kitchen as often as he'd been in his own.

As the stew began giving off the twin aromas of onion and garlic, Riley handed her a glass of Cabernet. "Here's to—"

"If you turn this toast into something sentimental, I'll brain you with the wine bottle." She'd had enough crying for one night.

"Fair enough. Here's to the spirit of competition."

"I'll drink to that." She thought about the events she had lined up and smiled. "You are so beaten this year, Kinnard."

He took a sip of his wine. "You don't know what I have in my garage."

"No, but considering you've been working on yours for one afternoon, and I've been working on mine since last week, you're playing catch-up, and that's never a good position." She tasted the wine and then looked at the bottle. Out of the dozen she had lying in the rack, he'd picked her absolute favorite. Lucky guess.

He walked over and lifted the saucepan lid. "This is ready."

She thought he was entirely too comfortable in her space.

She wished he didn't fit in this kitchen even better than he had in the Faulkners'. She pictured them muddling through a recipe together and drinking wine to soften the blow if the meal turned ugly. They'd always had a good time together, which was why she'd had so much trouble finding someone else.

They had the food dished and more wine poured with a minimum of fuss. Riley even took time to scout out the matches and light the candles on the small table at the end of the kitchen. Then he did something totally unexpected. He held out her chair.

"I can't remember the last time a man did that," she said as she sat down. "Thank you."

"You have to remember that my mom is Southern. If she'd had her way, I would have grown up saying yes ma'm, but my dad prevailed so I wouldn't end up looking like a dweeb in school."

"I've always loved your mom's accent." Hayden discovered Riley had also located the cloth napkins, and she put hers in her lap. The stew smelled wonderful, and she dug into it.

"And she always loved you." Riley kept eating as if he weren't dropping conversational bombshells. It seemed that men could eat, no matter what. "My mom's never forgiven me for losing you."

Hayden's breathing hitched. "Does she know why that happened?"

"More or less." Riley spooned up another bite of stew. "I tried to explain, but I think she sided with you on it. She thought what I did was unforgivable."

Hayden gazed at him, her meal forgotten. "Please tell me you're not mounting some campaign to woo me because you want to please your mother."

"God, no." He picked up a piece of the toasted beer bread and glanced over at her. "Tell you what. Let's keep our parents out of this. Let's forget about your mother hating me and my mother blaming me for messing up a good thing. Let's just deal with us." He took a healthy bite of the bread.

"Okay." She remembered that feeling of solidarity they used to have—them against the world. Sure, they'd battle each other endlessly, but they'd formed a united front against everyone else. She missed that more than she was willing to admit.

Riley chewed and swallowed. "Here's what I'd like. I'd like you to listen—really listen—to what happened on graduation night."

Her stomach twisted. "Riley, if you're going to load me up with bullshit, then you can just—"

"Just listen." He laid a hand on her arm. "I've never had a chance to tell you my side without you interrupting and getting mad. I deserve that much."

She wasn't sure he deserved anything, but she had a tough time denying him when he gave her that soulful gaze with those killer green eyes. "All right. What you got?"

"I don't know if you'd noticed, but Lisa Trenton had been after me ever since she moved here our junior year."

Hayden felt the familiar bile rise in her throat. "Oh, I know, believe me. She wasn't subtle."

"But I never had anything to do with her."

"Until that party at Rob's house." The agony of it came rushing back as if it had happened yesterday. "Then you had a whole lot to do with her. For all I know, after I left you took her out to the back of your pickup, showed her a copy of *The Joy of Sex*, and—"

"No, damn it! No! She knew you were in the kitchen helping Rob's mom with the food. Her instincts were excellent, like some bird of prey. She also knew I'd had way too much of that spiked punch. I swear she staged it so you'd walk in at the exact moment she grabbed my hand, placed it on her boob, and pulled my head down for a kiss."

"And you hated it, didn't you? I could tell by the way you

leaned into her." Hayden knew she sounded bitchy and sarcastic, but that scene was burned into her mind, and Riley had not been resisting. If he hadn't wanted to kiss Lisa, he should have been resisting, damn it! He was ten times stronger than Lisa.

"Hayden, I was a little bit drunk, okay? She had an agenda, and she was on me before I had any idea what she had in mind. Her plan worked perfectly when you saw us together, because you told me off and broke up with me in front of all our friends."

She had done that. But she wasn't proud of the fact. She'd always had a dramatic streak, which was why she'd ended up in film school and made her living as a set designer. But the drama needed to stay on the set. Her only excuse for the scene she'd caused was that she'd only been eighteen.

She glanced over at him. "I embarrassed you."

"Big time."

"And I apologize for that, but if you hadn't—"

"Also, for your information, I had Kevin drive me home that night. Her plan fell apart after that first success, because I didn't seek comfort in her arms, as she probably had the thing scripted. We never dated, let alone had sex."

Hayden tended to believe him, but still… "If some woman can take advantage of you when you're a little bit drunk, what does that mean? That you're faithful until someone shows up with a six-pack?"

"Hayden, I was *eighteen.* Can you give me a little credit for maturing since then?"

She'd held on to this grudge for a long time. She wasn't sure how to let it go.

"Jesus, but you're stubborn." Riley pushed back his chair and his gaze had turned brittle. "I've had my say. Maybe you're right. Maybe it's too late to mend that fence."

"All I know is, it can never be the same."

"Right! But did it ever occur to you that it could be even better?" He stomped out of the kitchen.

"Don't you want your cheesecake?"

"Nope! You can have your cheesecake and eat it, too. I have a Christmas display to work on." The door didn't quite slam, but it didn't click softly closed, either. Riley was obviously pissed in the way only a hot-blooded Irishman could be pissed.

She might have a flair for drama, but he was no slouch at creating his own. His exit line had been delivered with relish. Oh, yeah, Riley had enjoyed stomping off in a huff.

So let him. Did he imagine that one quick explanation would make her leap into his arms and declare her undying devotion? He might have been drunk when Lisa grabbed him, but he'd still been wrong not to put up some resistance. She hadn't heard him apologizing for not doing that.

In fact, Hayden had been the one apologizing for making a scene! What the hell? He'd started the whole debacle by allowing Lisa to kiss him. She'd reacted the way any girl in love would react.

And she still loved him, she realized. That was the real explanation for the waterworks during sex. She hadn't felt like admitting it, though. What sort of idiot kept loving someone for ten years? Sure, she'd slept with other guys, but she'd never given any of them her heart. It wasn't hers to give. Riley had it.

Fortunately he didn't know that, which meant she could salvage some of her pride. She could also put up the best damned Christmas display this street had ever seen. Grabbing the wine bottle, she walked into the darkened living room and looked through the picture window at the house across the street.

A sliver of light shone under the closed garage door, and the muffled sound of a power saw seeped through the crack. If Riley could work on his display at night, so could she.

She took a gulp of wine, drinking straight from the bottle like a gunslinger from the Wild West. This showdown would be wild, all right. She'd planned on a slow escalation over several nights, but she'd abandoned that strategy. Tomorrow night she'd hit him with everything she had.

RILEY'S SECOND INTERVIEW ran late, and the interview team invited him to join them for lunch. Much as he wanted to get home and keep working on his Christmas display, he couldn't risk turning down that invitation. It had been the right move. They'd offered him the job.

That lunch coupled with an extra supply run to Home Depot meant he didn't get home until after three. He wasn't surprised to see a horse trailer in Hayden's driveway. She'd made great strides in her display, too. Everything looked pretty much done, with lights strung everywhere and pine boughs and wreaths all over the bunkhouse and corral.

He wondered if she realized the horses would eat anything within reach once they were turned into that tiny corral. She'd had a dog and two cats as a kid, but he couldn't remember her ever going through a horse phase.

Well, it wasn't his problem what the horses did, or what she'd do with the horse poop, or whether she'd even thought to get a permit to have those animals in her yard. He knew the zoning didn't permit horses. When he'd turned ten and had thought he wanted to be a cowboy, he'd checked.

Damon Claus's truck was parked in front of the Faulkners' house, and Damon was stringing lights on the cactus. Every once in a while, a swear word floated over on the slight breeze. Decorating cactus was not a fun job.

Riley had called Damon on his cell to postpone their work schedule, so Damon had said he'd use the extra time to complete the Faulkners' yard.

Damon glanced up when Riley climbed out of the car. "Be

right with you, man!" he called over. "Did you get a load of what's going on across the street? Stiff competition over there. I talked to her, and she's out to annihilate you."

"Let her try." Riley hadn't been up half the night for nothing. He had three half-horsepower motors in the trunk. Once his display revved up, no one would care to look at a couple of horses in a corral and a quaint old bunkhouse.

Thanks to his psychology minor, he knew he was subli-mating his sexual needs by putting up this outrageous con-struction. If Hayden had seen fit to offer the olive branch last night, which would have led to them getting horizontal again—maybe even a third time, although his stamina wasn't quite as good as it had been at eighteen—he wouldn't be pulling out all the stops on this yard display.

Then again, he might have pulled out most of the stops, regardless. He did have that competition gene. But he wouldn't have been quite so driven to grind her into the dust. Damn it, why couldn't she just put the past behind her and look at what they could have in the present? She was making such a big deal out of such a small thing.

"Ready to go to work?" Damon sauntered over from the Faulkners' yard. He was sporting small bandages on both hands.

Riley glanced at the bandages. "Are you up to it?"

"Hell, yeah. But that cactus bites."

"You sound surprised." Riley had suspected Damon had very little experience in the Christmas decorating business.

"They don't have cactus where I come from."

"And where's that?"

"Up north."

Riley decided not to push it. He had a feeling whatever Damon said would be an approximation of the truth, anyway. For all Riley knew, Damon was on the run from the law. But he was here now, and Riley needed another pair of hands, bandaged or not.

Two hours later, they'd finished, and just in time, too. The light was fading fast, and soon they'd have trouble seeing what they were doing. Besides, Riley had wanted to light up the display tonight, because he sensed that Hayden was about to do the same.

Damon stood back to look at the Chicago skyline portrayed in plywood. Riley joined him. Hands planted at his hips, he took a deep breath. It was damned good, and his parents, who'd had a great time visiting him in Chicago over the years, were going to love it.

The display stood twelve feet tall at the highest point, which was the Hancock building, and everything was wired so that once the switch was thrown, the skyscraper windows would appear lit. A Ferris wheel that actually turned was located at the end of Navy Pier, and yards of rumpled blue plastic suggested the waters of Lake Michigan. A second motor would send a little lighted tour boat over the plastic waves.

But it was the third moving part that Riley was counting on to blow away the competition, aka Hayden Manchester.

"Gonna fire it up?" Damon asked.

"Absolutely."

"Before you do, what's the deal with you and Hayden, anyway? I keep sensing these weird vibes."

"She's just a friend."

"Don't give me that crap, Kinnard. It's more than that. You just put up the freaking Hancock Building, man, which is so phallic it's scary. Meanwhile she's creating this homey little bunkhouse, which is like a nest, or a woman's—"

"Okay, I get your point. I'll admit we have some history going on."

Claus hung his shades on the neck of his T-shirt. "Did you ever see any of those old John Wayne and Maureen O'Hara movies?"

"I guess. On reruns. Why?"

"That's how I see you two. Always trying to get the upper hand. But that's okay. It makes the sex that much better, and I'm all for good sex."

Riley gazed at him. "Don't you think this conversation is a little inappropriate for a Christmas decorations guy to be having with his client?"

"Not really. See, on the side, I promote couples getting together for great sex, and in this case, I sort of combined the two objectives, so—"

"What the hell are you, some sort of X-rated matchmaker?"

Claus grinned. "I like that. That's a very good description of my side business. So what I'm saying is, I hope she likes your Hancock Building."

# 6

TAKING A PAGE out of Walt Disney's schematics for Disneyland, Hayden had scaled down her bunkhouse and corral. Therefore they fit the miniature horses she'd contracted to use during the hours the display would be live. The zoning department had assured her that they could make an exception for miniature horses, which were no bigger than Great Danes, after all, and she wasn't planning to keep them permanently on her property, anyway. It had helped that a friend from high school worked in the zoning department.

She had everything pretty much ready to go by late afternoon, except for Pete Gibson, her singing cowboy. She'd found his card tucked in her door, although he claimed not to have put it there.

If Pete wanted to be coy about that, she didn't care. He was perfect for her escalation strategy. Before Riley had arrived in town and challenged her to a Christmas display duel, she'd planned on using CDs of country Christmas carols, but now that wasn't good enough.

The singing cowboy wasn't just any guy. He was also someone she'd known in high school who worked construction during the day and sang at a local resort's chuck wagon dinners on the weekends. In order to be a part of her display, he'd had to arrange for a weekend substitute at the resort.

She'd told him the substitute would work fine for her display on weekends, but Pete wasn't having any of that.

He'd had a crush on her in high school, and she was afraid he still had a crush, judging from his eagerness to accommodate her needs. If she'd had another option, she wouldn't have used him. But short of importing someone from L.A., Pete was her best bet.

Except he was late. He'd promised to arrive by five-thirty, and it was a quarter to six. She hesitated to throw the light switch and unload the miniature horses, because she wanted everything to happen at once, for maximum effect.

As she stood in the yard talking to the wrangler who had brought the horses, she could see the imposing outline of Riley's creation. She had to admit the Chicago skyline was a nice choice, considering that Riley had been living in Chicago and many Tucson people were Chicago transplants who would appreciate a taste of home. But she couldn't figure out any Christmas connection.

Maybe he was planning to do something with the lighting that would make it look like a Chicago Christmas. She should wait for the lights to come on before making a judgment. She wondered how much he knew about lighting. He was an architect, not a set builder, so he might be planning to install a few red and green floodlights and call it good. That was fine with her. She'd have the better display.

Then, as if her thoughts had conjured up the transformation, Riley's skyline came to life. Hayden didn't want to be blown away by the effect, but she was. She'd been to Chicago a few times, and standing here, she could almost imagine herself on a harbor cruise watching the Ferris wheel turn at the end of Navy Pier.

And here came the harbor cruise boat, gliding over the waves! It disappeared from sight behind the display, and returned to glide past again. Genius. She still didn't understand how Christmas worked into this display, but it was impressive, all the same.

Where the hell was her singing cowboy? She needed to

answer Riley's challenge, and she needed to answer it now. As she scanned the street, a silver Corvette turned off the main artery and started toward her. The cowboy singing business must pay better than she'd thought.

Pete parked the car, unfolded his long, gangly frame from the driver's seat and climbed out, Stetson in hand. Settling the hat on his head, he thumbed it back in what looked like a studied move. He gave her a cocky grin as he gestured toward the car. "How do you like my baby?"

Hayden winced at the blatant attempt to impress her with his ride. Apparently he'd never outgrown that high school mentality that a fast car guaranteed a willing woman.

But she didn't have it in her to be mean. "Nice," she said, although she didn't put a lot of emphasis on the word.

"Thought you'd like it. Picked it up yesterday."

"Wow." Dear God, she hoped he hadn't bought the car to show off specifically for her. That would be awful.

"After you shut down for the night, we can go for a spin." He leaned into the car and pulled out his guitar.

Hayden started to panic. This was going from bad to worse. As she was trying to decide how to handle his assumption that she was interested in him without ticking him off and causing him to leave, a plywood version of Santa and his reindeer rose over the Chicago skyline across the street. So *that* was how Riley tied in Christmas.

Pete followed the direction of her gaze. "Hey, that's neat."

It was neat, Hayden thought. Santa and the reindeer, including a red-nosed Rudolf, traversed the skyline and disappeared behind the buildings. Hayden waited for Santa to reappear. Instead, from behind the lighted display came the unmistakable sound of Riley swearing.

"Santa's effing stuck!" Crouched behind the display, Riley glared at Damon. "The sleigh's too heavy."

"It's not too heavy. The motor's not big enough. I said you needed a bigger motor."

"They didn't have one in stock, okay? This was the best I could do." Riley flipped the switch on the motor, which smelled like something was burning. "We have to lighten the load." He studied the apparatus that was supposed to rise up over the city of Chicago.

"Dump Santa." Damon sounded positively gleeful about that idea.

"We can't dump Santa. Santa's gotta be there. He's the man."

"Yeah, yeah, yeah. It's always *Santa* in the limelight, isn't it? Everybody loves Santa. Blah, blah, blah. I wish—"

"We'll take out a few reindeer. Nobody will notice." Riley started untying the harness he'd created out of nylon rope so he could cut out a couple of reindeer with the keyhole saw.

"Exactly." Damon got excited again. "And you can start with Rudolf. What a publicity hog he is! I've even caught that dude signing autographs, which is a trick when you have hoofs instead of hands, and I know for a fact he tried to be a guest on *Larry King*. He—"

"Excuse me?" Riley stopped fooling with the harness and stared at Damon. The guy had always been weird, but he was quickly going beyond weird to scary.

Damon blinked. Then he started to laugh. "Hey, that was a joke, man! I was just kidding around, pretending Rudolph was real."

"Look, don't take this wrong, but you need to get into a different line of work. The whole idea of Christmas seems to bring out your dark side. I don't think it's your holiday."

"You're telling me! But when you're born a Claus, you have to make the best of it."

"You think because your name is Claus that you have to be hooked up somehow with Christmas?"

"Well, *duh.*"

"Damon, that's bull." He repositioned the strand of lights attached to the reindeer, so he could use his saw without cutting any of the wires. "But if your name bothers you so much, you could get it legally changed."

"Changing my name wouldn't help. I'd still be…who I am."

"Now that's a profound statement." Riley sawed off three of the reindeer for good measure. One of them had to be Rudolf, because he was in the lead. There would be no red nose blinking on this display, after all. Maybe next year he could do that, after he'd bought a bigger motor.

"It's okay," Damon said. "I get my kicks where I can. Which reminds me, aren't you glad your folks won that cruise?"

"Of course I am. They've always wanted to take a cruise and I'm sure they're having fun."

"No, I mean, aren't you glad they're not here right now to interfere with that neighborly love project you've got going on?"

Riley made a face. "That's sort of dead in the water." He fastened the lights back in place and put a shortened harness on the remaining reindeer.

"Don't give up yet. Yes, she's terminally stubborn and yes, you're a little slow to take responsibility for your actions, but flawed people deserve great sex, too."

Riley finished attaching the harness. "Thanks for the vote of confidence."

"Oh, I'm more than a cheerleader. You two naughty people needed privacy, so I made sure your folks won the cruise."

Riley's hand was halfway to the switch on the motor. He pulled it back and turned to Damon. "You made sure they won? What the hell does that mean?"

"I can't give you all the details, but once in a while I like to claim a little credit for my work. Sending them on that cruise was brilliant, if I do say so."

Riley sighed. He'd thought Damon was a little strange, but he hadn't realized he was a total nutcase. The man needed help, and once Santa was launched, he'd figure something out. Maybe the guy ran out of money for his medication.

"I can tell you don't believe me," Damon said. "You think I'm crazy."

"Not crazy. That's a terrible word. But I think you need help. As soon as I—"

"I don't like this getting around, and I don't tell people as a rule, but I'm related to someone pretty famous."

Riley knew when he was in over his head. He needed to consult with somebody about this situation. The Faulkners had gone to a production of The Nutcracker, and he didn't feel close enough to any of the other neighbors to saddle them with something like this. Well, except for Hayden.

Screw Santa and his sleigh. Riley needed to go find Hayden and get some advice on the Damon situation before the guy totally wigged out.

Damon leaned closer. "The thing is, I spend the season looking for people on the naughty list. That would be you and your bodacious neighbor. See, I'm Santa Claus's brother."

Too late. The wigging out was now total. Riley really needed Hayden's moral support. "Of course you are." Riley stood. "What do you say we go tell Hayden about this? She'd want to know." He started around the end of the display.

Damon followed. "You think? I'm not sure she'd believe me. I wasn't sure you'd believe me, either, but you are Irish."

"And that's important why?"

"The Irish believe in the wee folk, so Santa's not all that much of a stretch. And it stands to reason he has siblings."

"Faultless logic. I— Hold on." Riley put out a hand to stop Damon's progress. "What the hell? Look over there. What do you see?"

"Someone's moving in on your territory, man. Looks like he's got mistletoe and knows how to use it."

"Pete Gibson." A red haze settled over Riley's brain. "He used to be a choir geek." *With a massive crush on Hayden.* "I don't like the looks of this."

"You weren't supposed to."

Riley spared Damon a glance. "What do you mean?"

Damon laughed and started toward his truck. "Amazing how effective a business card stuck in a door can be. I think my work here is done."

"Hang on a minute. Don't leave. I'll be right back, and we'll see about getting you some help after I handle this problem across the street."

"I'd advise you to hot-foot it over there, man."

Riley spun around, and sure enough, Pete was kissing Riley's girl. And damn it, she was letting him do it. The engine on Damon's truck revved up, but Riley didn't have time to fool with the nutty guy. He had urgent business across the street.

HAYDEN HADN'T seen the kiss coming. They'd been discussing the music selection when suddenly Pete produced a sprig of mistletoe and swooped in. The kiss was wet and sloppy with a liberal use of tongue.

The shock of it froze her up for a second, which was enough time for Pete to drop the mistletoe and wind his long arms around her, pinning her arms to her sides so she couldn't push him away. She could bite him, but that would mean no singing cowboy for her display.

However, the longer he kissed her, the more she favored a CD player. She was about to chomp down on his tongue when she heard Riley's voice.

"I have to admit this is some display." Riley sounded out of breath and displeased. Extremely displeased.

Pete must've heard the warning in Riley's voice. He stepped back and glanced at the man looming over them. He and Riley were about the same height, but Riley's broad shoulders made him look a lot bigger.

Pete laughed nervously. "Oh, hey, Riley! I heard you were back in town for a while. It's good to see you again. I—"

Riley held up a hand, silencing him. Then he turned to Hayden, his features rigid. "You didn't tell me you were seeing Pete Gibson."

"I'm not."

"Then what the hell was that about?"

Hayden couldn't believe the irony. She gazed at him calmly, wondering if he'd pick up on it. "Nothing, Riley. Pete got a little carried away, is all."

"Are you two still together?" Pete asked.

"No," Hayden said, staring at Riley.

"Yes," Riley said, staring right back.

A tremor of excitement ran through her. "Since when?"

"Since we were three years old and you whacked me with that toy dump truck."

Hayden smiled. She knew how this story went. "And you started to cry."

"Yeah." Riley's expression softened. "And you kissed me."

"Because I couldn't bear to watch you cry."

Riley stepped closer. "Seeing you with Pete was much worse than a dump truck upside the head. And that's what you had to deal with ten years ago. I'm sorry, Hayden. I'm so, so sorry I let that happen."

Joy coursed through her. He got it. Finally. "You're not crying, though."

"Yeah, I am. On the inside. I desperately need a kiss. Several, in fact. Come to think of it, I'll probably need a bunch of kisses."

"Oh, Riley." She gazed at him in wonder as all the bitterness flowed away. "You were only eighteen."

"And stupid."

"So was I. I've held on to that grudge for way too long."

"Listen, Hayden," Pete said. "When do you want me to start singing? You said you wanted to blow Riley out of the water with your display."

"I've changed my mind about that." Hayden moved into Riley's arms. "I'd rather blow him out of the water with a kiss."

"I love you so much," he murmured. "And I'm sorry about Lisa. I behaved like an ass."

"And I behaved like a diva. I love you, too, Riley."

"Good thing." He cupped her cheek. "Because I landed the job, so it looks as if you'll have me around for a while."

"Is this your devious plan to get your hands on that model of the *USS Arizona?*"

"No, it's my devious plan to get my hands on you." And he kissed her so thoroughly that she decided they might want to take the party inside.

Much later as she lay snuggled in his arms, she thought about her belief that things would never be the same between them. Sure enough, things weren't the same. As it turned out, they were even better.

# HER SECRET SANTA
## Jill Shalvis

# 1

*Thanksgiving Day*

IT SHOULD HAVE BEEN the scent of pumpkin pie assaulting her senses, but instead, she was surrounded by the smell of scorched wood and melted steel. Arson investigator Ally Dauer carefully scanned the burned-out shell of what had only yesterday been a home improvement warehouse.

And then she found it. *"Gotcha,"* she murmured, crouching down for a better view of the dark triangle burn spot on the concrete floor.

A spot she'd be willing to bet was the origin of the fire.

She'd pulled on disposable gloves so as not to destroy evidence, but there was nothing to do about her clothes at the moment. Having been called away from Thanksgiving dinner with her parents, siblings, aunts, uncles and cousins, she still wore her little black dress and favorite black heels.

The Dauers dressed for Thanksgiving.

They also fought, a lot. Except this year, she'd actually made it through the pre-dinner social hour and then meal itself without being tempted to use the gun she was licensed to carry. Then she'd been paged just before dessert, the best part of the evening.

That had sucked.

Promising herself a run for ice cream when she was done, she lifted the digital camera from around her neck and began snapping away while attempting to keep her dress down far enough on her thighs so as not to flash any of the other fire personnel around her.

"Excuse me, Ms. Dauer?"

"Yes?" She glanced over at a tall, well-built man. Ageless. Dark hair, dark eyes. Wearing black trousers and a blue button up, looking like he'd been trying for office casual, but not even the respectable clothes could hide the edgy, slippery air around him.

That was odd.

She was on a fire scene, and possibly a crime scene, as well. No one was allowed but personnel, but she didn't recognize this guy. Her job was half-firefighter, half-cop, and the cop part of her kicked in now. "Who are you?"

"Damon Claus," he said, quickly flashing a department badge. "I just wanted to let you know that your toy drive has been shifted from your jurisdiction to mine."

It took her a minute to shift gears, going from an arson investigation to…toys. The annual toy drive was an unofficial part of her job. And since the official part of her job revolved around bad guys doing bad shit, she'd really been looking forward to the toy drive. "Why?"

Damon lifted a shoulder, noncommittal.

She narrowed her eyes, unwilling to concede. She loved Christmas, or at least the idea of it. Making sure every kid in Santa Rey had a gift was a mission she'd wanted. "I don't recognize you. What do you do again?"

"Toy director."

At that she laughed, relieved. Brushing off her hands, she stood up and looked around. "You at it again?" she yelled out to an invisible prankster. "I've been here six months already!" Determined to ignore the on-going hazing that came with being the lone woman in a sea of men, she went back to work, ignoring "Damon Claus." When he'd walked off, she once again lost herself in the work, shifting through the melted metal and blistered paint for more clues, alternating between taking notes and pictures.

It was definitely arson, she eventually decided, looking at this like she always did, like a puzzle that needed solving. Fires like this, hell most fires, did not start on their own. She already knew, from her initial research, that the company that owned this warehouse had been struggling financially for nine months. This was their third warehouse to have an unexplained fire.

She had no doubt that the insurance company would cry foul and launch their own investigation, as well.

Ally walked through the rest of the warehouse and out the back, where there were rows and rows of building material, most of it destroyed. The economic down turn had pretty much crashed and burned the building industry here in Santa Rey.

Then, out of the corner of her eyes, she caught a flash of movement. A small man, she thought, or maybe a teenager. "Hey," she called out. "This is a crime scene—"

The crack of a gun being fired answered her, and then the resounding *ping* of the bullet finding a home over her head in the steel frame of the warehouse behind her as she dove for cover.

At this rate, she was never going to get dessert!

When she heard running footsteps, she tossed aside her camera, pulled her gun from her thigh holster, and took off after the man, yelling behind her for back up in the form of Tommy, her boss, the head of Arson Unit.

She caught sight of her perp at the far back corner of the yard. He was limping, and swearing and sweating as he tripped over something and hit the ground hard.

Definitely a teenager.

She'd just about reached him when he leapt up and attempted to climb the chain link fence. He got about three feet up when she yanked him to the ground and put a knee to the small of his back.

By then, Tommy had come jogging up, tossing her a pair of handcuffs. "Nice," he said, yanking the perp to his feet. "But it was my turn to have the fun." He looked at the kid. "You start this fire?"

"No, I swear!"

Tommy turned to Ally, who shrugged. They both knew that most arsonists returned to the scene of the crime. But if this warehouse had burned for the money factor, the kid didn't exactly fit the profile.

Frowning, Ally let Tommy handle the situation and made her way back to where she'd left her camera and squatted down. Pulling her gun on the kid—even if he'd been the one to fire a shot—was going to mean extra paperwork and explanations, which didn't improve her mood. "Damn," she murmured, eyeing the cracked lens. Another one bit the dust. Then she went still as a prickle of awareness slid down her spine.

Two steel-toed black boots stepped into her field of vision.

Her gaze slid up, *way* up, past long, long legs, and then a torso covered in protective fire fighting gear, all six feet two inches of the body covered in soot and grime.

And even so, he was *still* the most deadly sexy guy she'd ever been dumped by.

Eddie Weston.

Slowly he crouched at her side until they were eye level. Though she knew he'd been up all night battling the fire, there was an alertness to him, a quiet stillness that other men seemed to lack.

His movements were fluid as he reached out and pulled something from her hair.

A few ashes.

His hand extended again, strong and calloused as his finger ran over her jaw. If she hadn't been rendered stupid by his nearness, she had been now, thanks to the visceral spark that had just zinged through her body.

Damn him.

Six months ago, when she'd first transferred to Santa Rey from Los Angeles, they'd gone out exactly twice. On the second date, they'd shared a couple of bone-melting kisses and a tantalizing hint of what the rest of the night could have been like before she'd been paged to go into work.

After that night, and in spite of herself and her policy of keeping work separate from pleasure, she'd started to fall for him.

Then nothing.

He'd never called her again.

It wasn't entirely unexpected. He and the guys at firehouse #34 had a fairly wild—and well-earned—reputation. Eddie wasn't a heartbreaker necessarily, but neither had he shown any signs of being a keeper.

She wasn't, either, though she wanted to be. Problem was, her job tended to scare men off. She worked a lot, and she faced a considerable amount of danger. Most guys couldn't take the pressure…or the intimidation.

Translation—she tended to get dumped.

She and Eddie ran into each other on the job frequently—her with her attitude, and him with the best ass in Santa Rey. Though there was always heavy flirting on his part and heavy whimsical inner desire on hers, nothing ever came of it.

And since she'd choke on her pride before asking him what the hell, she'd kept her cool.

At least on the outside.

As for Eddie, he was always cool. Simply put, he was the most startlingly, stunningly cool, laid-back, easy-going, sexy man she'd ever met.

His teeth flashed white against his dirty face. "Hey, cutie," he said, breaking the silence. "Nice tackle."

*Cutie?* Well, why didn't he just pat her on the head? "Thanks." She stared at her camera. Her broken camera. She'd really liked this one, too.

Still crouched at her side with knees splayed, he braced his elbows on them and dipped his face to see more clearly into hers, his eyes warm and curious.

His nearness did something warm and curious to her insides. Specifically the parts of her that were clamoring for a man's touch. "Can I help you with something?" she asked in her most professional voice.

"No. I just like watching you work."

Maybe that was true, but if so, he was alone in that enjoyment. Most guys were intimidated by her work.

Hence her dateless status.

Her orgasm-less status.

She met his gaze, and what she found there was something that made her forget about her broken camera.

Heat.

So much that she had to purposely let out a breath and then just as purposely draw another.

He'd had his chance!

Like his smile, his startling blue eyes stole her breath. He had fine lines fanning out from them, not from age but from squinting into the sun.

Yeah, he was sexy as hell.

And irritating.

"Did you catch the perp's face when he realized he was taken down by a woman?" He laughed. "God, it was great. *You* were great, Ally."

He had a nice laugh, all low and husky, and with his easy, genuine approval, she felt a funny quiver in her belly. "Thanks. Look, I'm pretty busy here. Got some evidence, and a teenager to question." *So if you could go before I beg you to ask me out one more time...*

Eddie craned his head and took in the sheer destruction around them. He and his partner Sam, along with their entire unit from Firehouse #34, had battled the blaze all night long. He had to be exhausted. "I just wanted to remind you. The toy drive started this week. I already have a box of stuff at the station, so I'll bring them by your office."

He was the firefighter assigned to help her with the drive? And that reminded her. "Do you know anything about a Damon Claus? He's new."

Eddie shook his head. "Never heard of him. Besides, how can he be new? We're on a hiring freeze."

Huh. Very true. Then what he'd just said sank in. He was going to come to her office, probably looking like sin on a stick. "Listen, you don't have to bring the toys. I'll come get them."

*On another day. When you're off duty.*

"That's not how it works," he said. "It's my job to pick all the contributions from the stations every week and bring them to you. Your job is to distribute them."

"Oh." She could handle this, handle seeing him a few extra times this month. She'd just strap on her big girl panties and ignore the fireworks she felt whenever he was near her.

He was watching her, apparently reading her hesitation. Just as apparently, it amused him. "You looked thrilled to be seeing me once a week. Don't worry, Ally, we'll keep it painless."

He needed to speak for himself.

Then he leaned in close, surprising her. But he simply ran a finger over her shattered camera lens. "A damn shame. It was a nice SLR."

"You know cameras?"

"I do. I even have one just like this one, if you want to borrow it until you replace yours."

His radio squawked, and she heard his captain's voice calling him back to his rig. Reaching out, he tweaked her ponytail and smiled as he straightened up, offering her a hand to do the same. "Take it easy out here. Stay safe."

"Thanks," she murmured, craning her neck to watch him walk away. Yeah, he was dangerous to her mental health and she needed to keep clear. But hell, she wasn't blind. Even in his fire fighter uniform, even covered with soot and grime, she wasn't going to pass up an opportunity to watch his butt as he walked away.

With a sigh that might have been a little dreamy, she headed back inside to continue her investigation.

When she was gone, a tall, dark shadow stepped out from behind one of the aisles of building material.

Damon Claus.

His hands were in his pockets, his eyes covered in his Ray-Ban sunglasses, his mouth tight. Christmas spirit pissed him off. And little Miss Hot and Sexy Fire Investigator might be tough-as-nails, but that tough-as-nails shell hid a huge, fiercely loyal heart, one with Christmas spirit in abundance.

He knew that unless he tripped her up somehow, she was going to make this year's toy drive the most successful yet, spreading that Christmas spirit like wild fire.

He needed a distraction.

And as he watched her watch Eddie Weston as he headed toward his rig, Damon thought he might just have found one.

# 2

THE NEXT MORNING, Eddie dragged his ass out of the station shower, favoring his left leg. He shoved his fingers through his short brown hair, pulled on civilian clothes in the form of beloved old jeans and a shirt, and called it good.

His long time partner and best friend Sam Reed watched him limp across the locker room. "You should have gotten that checked out, man."

"It's better." At three in the morning, they'd been called to a house fire. Eddie had been on the roof when it'd collapsed, sending him sliding through to the ground floor. To come out with only a single bruise and a four inch gash had been a miracle. "I'm good."

Sam just raised a brow as Eddie limped to a chair to slip on his shoes. "Sure?"

"Yeah. Go home to your other wife, the one who likes it when you fuss."

Sam got a goofy grin on his face at the mention of his new wife, Sara. "You know the best part of being married?"

"Uh, getting laid every night?"

Sam laughed. "Yeah."

Not so long ago, the two of them had been partners in crime when it came to the women of Santa Rey, Eddie thought, shaking his head. He grabbed his keys and headed out, blinking in the bright, early morning sun.

He didn't have a wife to go home to, nor a girlfriend, though for the first time in his life, he wouldn't have minded, either. The air was chilly, and as he looked across the street to the gorgeous, empty beach, at the waves crashing onto the sand. He breathed in the salty air and wished he had his surfboard.

And a wetsuit.

But even he, who'd been surfing since he could walk, wasn't ready to risk his neck in winter. Unless he was in Hawaii...

It wasn't happening this year. He and his sisters and brothers had just sent their parents on an anniversary cruise to Mexico, and since two out of the four siblings hadn't been able to come up with their share, he'd forked the extra cash over. Plus, he'd been slowly renovating the fixer upper he'd bought last year, using cheap manual labor—his friends and siblings. As much as he'd kill to go to Hawaii, he simply couldn't afford it.

Giving the high surf one last longing look, he turned to his truck, yawning as he limped in. The EMTs had cleaned his leg up and he'd wrapped it but it hurt like a SOB, throbbing with each heartbeat. For a minute, he sat in his truck with his head back, eyes closed. He'd just spent four straight days on duty, with no less than five calls each night.

Why the hell couldn't people have their emergencies in the middle of the damn day?

And his day wasn't his own, at least not yet. But at least what came next was something he was looking forward to.

Seeing Investigator Ally Dauer again.

It took him an hour to hit each of the other three fire stations in town, gathering up the toys donated so far for the toy drive. Finally, he headed to the fire department's head-quarters with his loot, making a quick stop for two coffees and a couple of donuts, having the feeling that a bribe might come in handy.

He put his SLR digital camera in the box with the toys,

stacked the coffees and donut bag on top and ambled into headquarters. It was early but he knew Ally would be in her office. She worked hard, straddling her two worlds—part-cop, part-firefighter. She was good at what she did, and gave the job her all. As far as he knew, she gave *everything* her all—she didn't appear to know any other way.

It was sexy as hell. *She* was sexy as hell.

Memories of last night came back to him, seeing her fear-lessly racing across the crime scene in that hot little black dress and high heels, gun in hand like a Bond girl as she'd gone after that punk kid. The way she'd looked holding her perp to the ground, her knee in his back, cuffing him, had given him more than a few X-rated dreams.

In fact, he had an entire file in his brain labeled: *Hot Fantasies Starring Ally Dauer.* He accessed that mental file now, taking out one of his favorites, which involved her and those handcuffs and—

"Hiya, sweet cheeks," said Cherry, the floor's reception-ist. She was pert and pretty, and waving at him. Obliging, he moved closer to her desk. She leaned over it, giving him a nice view down her top to her breasts, which were as pert and pretty as the rest of her. "Going to be at the poker party this weekend?" she asked.

This weekend he'd be painting the master bathroom in his house. "Sorry."

"Aw, it's like the changing of an era. Sam got married, and you bought that house and got all domesticated," she said sadly.

Yeah, he had. And he liked it. No more waking up hung-over, sometimes alone, sometimes not, but always…rest-less.

"Maybe next time?" Cherry asked hopefully.

"Maybe. Is Ally Dauer in?"

"Just got here."

"Thanks." He lugged the box and his bribe down the hall, stopping in her doorway. As always, the sight of her gave him a one-two punch. Partly because she was hot, and partly because…hell. He had no clue. She wasn't even his type. She tended to be anal and driven.

But apparently there was no reasoning with chemistry.

She was behind her desk, her strawberry-blond hair pulled back in its usual neat ponytail, a little pair of reading glasses perched on her nose and a pencil between her teeth as she tapped away on a laptop and simultaneously spoke on the phone.

And just like that, another fantasy raised its dirty head— the naughty secretary.

She was talking about the teenager she'd caught on scene yesterday, telling someone that just because he was a stupid kid in the wrong place at the wrong time didn't excuse the fact that he'd had a gun he'd stolen from his friend's father. Or that he'd used it. Her point made, she hung up and noticed Eddie standing there.

"Hey," he said with a smile.

Her haze eyes narrowed and she didn't say a word.

Clearly, she was crazy about him.

But he knew the way to her heart. Setting down the box of toys on a spare chair, he handed her his camera.

Sure enough, she gasped and hugged it to her chest.

"Funny, I've never been jealous of a camera before," he chuckled.

She ignored that. "Eddie, I can't borrow this." Even as she said it, she gripped it tight like she wasn't going to let it go. "I have a bad track record with—"

"I trust you." Next, he handed her one of the coffees. Taking the other, he sat across from her.

She let out a sigh, along with some of her tension, took a sip of her coffee, then eyed the donut bag.

He handed it over.

Peeking in, she finally let loose a smile and a hum of pleasure that sounded so sexual, his dick twitched.

She pulled out the chocolate old-fashioned glazed donut and stared at it all soft-eyed. "Well, hello, lover," she cooed. At her first bite, she moaned load and throaty. "Oh my God."

Eddie watched her suck some chocolate off her thumb and had to remind himself to breathe. He liked the way she looked all devoid of tension. He liked it a lot. He took a cherry-filled donut and they ate in companionable silence, him still hard as a rock, her still looking like she was a fraction of an inch from orgasm.

He polished off his within minutes and eyed hers.

She still had half left.

She noticed him looking at it, then held it out to him— only to pull it back when he reached for it. "Sweet Cheeks?" she murmured.

"Huh?"

She arched a brow. "Cherry. She called you sweet cheeks."

He let out a breath and shrugged. He wasn't going there. It was embarrassing.

She just looked at him, then swiveled her finger in an unmistakable demand for him to stand up and turn around.

"Seriously?"

She just gave a pointed glare at the half donut in her fingers and baiting him, took another *slooooow* bite.

With a shake of his head, he stood, turned, and gave her a view of his ass. When he faced her again, she handed him the rest of her donut. "Nice, but I don't know about sweet."

"I didn't make up the nickname."

She licked the pad of her thumb to get the last little bit of chocolate, then sucked it into her mouth with an enthusiasm that went straight through him. "But I noticed you didn't ask her to *stop* calling you sweet cheeks."

He wasn't vain, but neither was he stupid. Yes, he knew women found him attractive. Hell, he'd spent nearly all of his twenties exploiting that very fact. "Would you feel better if I filed a sexual harassment case?"

"You?" She rolled her eyes. "I was worried about Cherry. I like her. And I'd hate to see you play her."

"Play her," he repeated.

She went back to her computer. "It's just that if you're going to date her twice and then drop her like a bad habit, maybe you could just spare her and back off now."

He stared at her. "Okay, call me slow, but are we still talking about Cherry?"

"Forget it."

"No. You're mad at me."

"I'm not mad."

"I grew up with three sisters," he said. "I know women. You're mad."

She snorted and went back to typing, which was irritating, even if she was hot. Leaning in, he closed her laptop, leaving his hand on top of it. They were close now, close enough that he could press his face into her sweet smelling hair if he wanted, or to her neck, which would be even nicer.

She lifted her gaze to his and he caught a glimpse of the same almost bewildered attraction he felt. Damn, her glasses even magnified her eyes, which were fathomless and completely unreadable. "Talk to me, Ally."

She drew a shaky breath. "Why are you limping?"

"I fell through a roof. Why are you mad at me?" he repeated quietly.

Standing, nearly bumping into his body with hers, she declined to answer and walked to the box he'd brought, and began looking through the unwrapped toys. "Wow. Great start," she said, sounding genuinely pleased. "The kids are going to love—" Breaking off, she frowned and pulled out a box, wrapped in shiny red paper covered with naked Santas. "What the—"

He looked at it, and with a laugh, shook his head. "I don't know. Someone's idea of funny?"

"It's inappropriate, is what it is." Then her eyes narrowed. "There's a tag."

Shifting closer, he read over her shoulder: *To: Fire Investigator Ally Dauer.*

Their gazes met.

Held.

"You must have an admirer," he said.

"Is his name Eddie Weston?"

Trick question alert. "I'm an admirer," he said carefully. "But no, I didn't do this."

She just looked at him for a long moment, as if searching for honesty. When he shrugged, she ripped off the paper. Then she went utterly still.

"What?"

She held up a small specialty bottle. "Flavored massage oil."

Huh. He wasn't crazy about the thought of someone sending her a gift like that, especially in this manner, secretly and sneakily. He wasn't sure how he felt about her, or what he wanted from her, but he did know this. For whatever reason, he was definitely drawn to her. He had been from the beginning, and he wanted her safe.

She read the label and grimaced. "Sensual, self-heating." Her cheeks were pink. "Um."

"What?"

"It's…edible."

The air between seemed to crackle. Yep, he was definitely drawn to her. Which made it all the more frustrating that she'd not shown any interest in him. They could have had something pretty damn hot together. "How thoughtful," he finally said. "Boyfriend maybe?"

"No. None."

"Stalker?"

"Not this week."

"Good." He smiled, not sure what it said about him that he was more relieved about her lack of boyfriend than lack of stalker. He moved close, taking the bottle from her hand. "Peach flavored," he murmured, thinking hot peach pie, slathered over smooth, creamy skin. Oh, yeah. His favorite dessert.

"Who would send this to me?" she asked.

She didn't sound particularly steady, and he wondered if her reaction had more to do with whatever the hell seemed to be happening between them today, or with the present. "I'm taking it you have no contenders?"

She opened her mouth, then closed it, apparently figuring no answer was the best way to go.

He took her hand and poured a drop in her palm, then lifted it to his mouth, touching his tongue to the very center of her palm.

She jerked and stared at him. "It's heating up!"

"Uh-huh." And that wasn't the only thing heating up. He had more than one body part doing the same. When he sank his teeth into the fleshy part of her hand, she gasped in a breath.

"Eddie." She simply stood there, eyes a little wide, mouth a little open, her nipples pressing against her shirt.

He ran the pad of his thumb over her knuckles and shifted closer, breathing out her name as her eyes slowly drifted closed—

"Eddie? Line one," Cherry called from down the hall. "It's station thirty-one. You forgot to pick up their box of toys."

He didn't take his eyes off Ally. "Tell them I'm coming."

In front of him, Allie swallowed. Nodded. "You're coming—" She grimaced. "I mean going. You're going—" She slapped one hand over her eyes, then used the other to give him a not-so-gentle shove toward the door.

He resisted and pressed his mouth to her ear. "I'd rather be coming."

With a soft, indistinguishable sound, she gave him one last push out of her office.

And then for good measure, she slammed the lock home with a loud click.

Yep. She was crazy about him.

# 3

ALLY SPENT the rest of the week resolutely *not* thinking about how at the touch of Eddie's tongue to her palm, heat had slashed through her.

Okay, she thought about it.

A lot, but she was only human.

And that's what made her so damn cautious with men. She had no trouble attracting them, but she sure as hell had trouble keeping them. Yes, she was focused on her work, but she could focus on more than one thing at a time.

Or she wanted to think she could.

But a relationship hadn't been in the cards for her. As a result, she knew she'd built a wall around herself, keeping the vicious cycle going.

At least she loved her work. She was finishing up a long, tough drawn-out investigation that she and the arson department had been working on for five months. The fires had caused six deaths, two of them children. But finally, they'd been able to nail their bad guy. She'd been there for the arrest, and felt the surge of satisfaction of a job well done.

But she'd been putting in long hours and was exhausted. Unfortunately, she still had a stack of paperwork threatening to take over her desk. And on the top was a full file with a burgeoning set of notes she'd tentatively labeled:

*Her Secret Santa.*

She'd kept the massage oil and the wrapping paper for

evidence. The paper and a Polaroid of the oil was in the file. She'd looked up the adult novelty stores in the area and intended to check out the kind of merchandise each of them handled.

Eyeing her To Do stack, she blew out a sigh. All she really wanted was some dinner, maybe a glass of wine, and at least eight hours horizontal. There'd been a time when she would have added a man-induced orgasm to the list but she thought she just might be too tired for even that.

Okay, so she'd stick around the office for another hour, get something done, then go home and collapse. That decided, she moved down the hall into the staff room for some caffeine, and was alternating sipping and blowing on the hot coffee when she walked back into her office.

And found a new box of toys on her chair.

In her line of work, instinct was critical, and she'd learned never to doubt hers. On a hunch, she immediately set down her coffee and pulled out the unwrapped toys. "Crap," she whispered, discovering the single wrapped gift in the bottom.

This time the paper was shiny green, but the naked Santas were the same. Grabbing the gift, she ran out the door towards the reception area, just in time to hear Cherry say to Eddie, "See ya, sweet cheeks."

Allie's jaw clicked tight. He was clearly off duty, in faded jeans, a soft white untucked henley and scuffed sneakers, looking better than a dead man walking had a right to look. "Hey, sweet cheeks," she said, and had the unexpected pleasure of watching Eddie wince as he turned to face her.

"Can I see you a moment. In my office?"

He looked at the present in her hands, clearly realized the implications, and his easy smile faded. His eyes, always watchful, went uncharacteristically serious. Something else sparked there, as well, something she couldn't quite put her finger on. At first glance she might have said protectiveness, but that was ridiculous given that he'd just moved to the top of her suspect list.

They walked side by side down the hall, her vibrating with awareness of being so close to him, all six feet two of warm, hard muscle. "You're not limping as badly today," she noted.

Apparently he had no response to that as he put a hand to her lower back, gently pushing her into her office ahead of him. "Open it," he said in his deep, even voice.

Feeling a catch in her chest, she stepped away from him. She'd discovered she couldn't think with his big, warm hand on her. Then she pulled off the paper and stared down at the book entitled *Even Losers Can Get Laid—Yes, I'm Talking To You*. She choked out a laugh that had no humor in it.

It hit a little too close to home…

There was a bookmark stuffed in the pages, of a stacked blonde wearing a Santa hat, long red gloves, red thigh-high stockings, and nothing else. The page that had been bookmarked was the first in a new chapter—*How To Kiss To Get Lucky*.

Eddie chuckled, a soft, low sound that scraped at her belly. Lifting her head, she narrowed her eyes. "This isn't funny. What the hell is this about?"

His eyes widened slightly in disbelief. "You think I sent it?"

"Well, hello, you're the one delivering the toys!"

He let out a long breath. "Okay, that does look bad, but here's the thing."

"The thing? What thing?"

He ran an agitated hand through his hair and looked like he'd rather have a tooth pulled without Novocain.

"Spill it, Weston."

"Both times I personally put all the toys in that box. The box was empty beforehand and it never left my sight. But I absolutely didn't give you either of those…*gifts*." He flashed a small smile. "Not that I can't appreciate the humor, but I already know you can kiss." Their eyes locked for a long moment. "And second, I couldn't have wrapped them that well."

She let out a breath and plopped down onto her desk, drumming her fingers on the opened Her Secret Santa file.

Eddie caught sight of the papers, and before she could stop him, picked up the file.

"Hey. Confidential information."

He simply held it too high for her to reach as he skimmed her notes, then slid her a look that said he was thinking about smiling. "An official investigation? Really?"

"Shh!" She shut her door, which only seemed to further amuse him. "And not *official* official." She rolled her eyes and looked away when he let out a low, delighted laugh.

"I want in on it," he said.

"No."

"Hell, yes." He leaned a hip on her desk, as if maybe his leg was still bothering him after all. "I'm already involved," he added. "I'm also a city official, same as you. So I'm in."

Her stomach growled, loudly, echoing in the room. She'd gone without lunch, and now it was well past dinner time. She was too hungry to be embarrassed, or even argue effectively.

He seemed to sense her weakened state and put the sex manual into the file folder, tucking it under his arm. With his free hand, he grabbed hers. "Come on."

"Where?"

"Just come on."

She didn't argue, which was really unlike her. She must be hungrier than she thought. She waited until he'd opened the passenger door to his truck for her, and then come around, carefully hoisting himself into the driver's seat. "Your leg—"

"Is fine."

"It doesn't seem like it."

"Do you need to see for yourself?"

They both knew that for her to do that, he'd have to pull down his pants. She was wrestling with the conflicting lust and terror of that thought when he laughed softly. "God, you should come play poker with us. I'd make a killing off you." Leaning over the console between them, he put his mouth to her ear and whispered, "And any time you want my pants off, Ally, all you have to do is ask."

She blushed, pretended she didn't care, and stared out the window while he chuckled softly at her embarrassment.

He drove them into town, parking in the lot in front of her favorite café.

"What are we doing?" she asked.

"I'm too hungry to think." He pulled her inside, nudged her into one of the back booths, then slid in beside her instead of across from her.

"Hey. My space."

"I like your space. Did you figure out if you want me to take off my jeans yet?"

"Yes. No!" She closed her eyes. "They stay on."

"Let me know if that changes." He was in close enough that his warm breath brushed her temple. "And as for me sitting next to you, it was for the discussion we're going to be having about hot massage oil, sex manuals and naked Santas. I thought you'd want a little discretion."

Yes, but she also wanted distance, from his big, bad, tough, gorgeous bod. With distance, she could remember that she'd been hurt and embarrassed by the fact that six months ago she hadn't been enough to hold his interest for more than two dates and she didn't think anything had changed there. Bottom line, she'd thought they could have had something…

Hell, she still thought it. Damn him.

He was slouched back, legs sprawled out in front of him, one long arm stretched out along the back of the booth behind her. He had shoved his sunglasses to the top of his head and had at least a day's growth of stubble growing on his strong jaw. He looked more than a little dangerous.

Luckily she already knew she was only in danger if she let down her guard—and that wasn't going to happen again.

Their waitress was young and cute and snapping a wad of bubble gum, which she almost swallowed when Eddie smiled at her. "What can I get you?" she practically purred.

He turned to Ally, a question in his gaze. "What sounds good?"

What sounded good? His voice. "Pizza."

"Pizza it is," he said. "And two beers."

The waitress beamed at him as if he'd just given her the moon, then she bounced off. Yes, bounced. Allie slid him a look. "Does that ever get old?"

"What?"

"The adoration?"

He smiled the smile of a man confident in his own skin. "No."

Rolling her eyes, Ally leaned back when the waitress brought their beers. She was a complete lightweight in the alcohol department but she had a feeling that tonight she'd need the fortification. She took a long pull, watching as Eddie did the same.

Then he set down his bottle, gave her a heavy-lidded look, and pulled open the sex manual to the bookmarked page. "Interesting."

Thinking he'd found something she'd missed, a clue of some kind, she leaned into him, trying to see what he was looking at. When she moved, his biceps brushed the side of her breast. And if that wasn't enough to send a bolt of sheer desire through her, he smelled warm and deliciously male. She ignored it all. "What? What did you find?"

"It says here the key to a hot kiss is to make it as similar to the sexual act itself as possible."

Oh, God. His voice was like a shot of whiskey. Low and smooth and potent. To distract herself, she took another long pull on her beer and slapped the bottle to the table.

His gaze went from the beer to her mouth, and he smiled. "It says that a kiss should be long and wet and deep, preferably with a slow glide of the tongue." He cocked his head and kept looking at her. "I like the slow glide part."

She remembered! Worse, her body remembered too. Her breasts felt…full. Her thighs were clenched, and between them, she felt an undeniable tingle.

"It also says that full body contact is suggested, from chest to groin to thigh."

He hadn't used a single obscene word and she'd gone damp. She squeezed her thighs and let out an indistinguishable sound that she covered by downing the last of her beer.

He was watching her carefully. "I think we're ready for the next chapter," he murmured. Then he started to read. "Getting from the kiss to the naked stage—"

He broke off when she slapped her hands over the pages. If he continued in that voice, she might have an orgasm on the spot. "We failed there."

His gaze searched her face. "Failed?"

"Okay, not we. Me. I failed."

He studied her a long moment. "Explain."

"We went out." Damn beer. Her tongue felt loose. "Twice."

"Yes."

"We kissed." She pointed to the book. "Long and deep and wet."

Now his lips curved and he sighed in fond memory. "Uh-huh."

"And then nothing. You never called me again. No naked."

He looked at her for a long moment. "You never gave me any indication that you wanted to go in that direction, or even that you wanted to see me again. In fact, when I walked you inside your place after our second date, you patted me on the shoulder and said you'd be real busy over the next couple of months but that it'd been real nice hanging out."

"And it had been nice."

"It felt like a brush off."

"No, it wasn't. It was me...trying to open up."

He shook his head in bafflement.

"I don't get it," she said. "I said it was nice. *Nice* is a perfectly good word, Eddie."

He looked at her as if she'd come from another planet. "*Nice* is the word you use to describe the guy you call when you need a tire changed. *Nice* is the man at the store who reaches something on the top shelf that you can't. *Nice* is for the neighbor who brings in your mail when you're out of town. *Nice* is *not* for the guy you want to go out with dancing until dawn and then come home and get naked and sweaty and have some wall-banging sex. *Nice* is *not* for the guy you want to take you to the mountains for screaming sex beneath the stars."

Oh my. Wall-banging sex?

Screaming sex?

God, all she could think was, *Yes, please*. Where did she sign up for that?

"Ally?"

She realized he was waving a hand in front of her face, and she jumped.

"You okay?"

"Yes," she said faintly.

Pay attention.

Distance.

They were both keys to a good, smart, effective investigation. "All of those traits," she said. "The car thing, the mail thing...I like them. I'd like them in a man."

"Yes, but they put a man decidedly in the 'friend' category."

"When I date someone, I want them to be a friend."

Still watching her, he took her hand. "So what are you

saying? That you would have kept going out with me as a friend, or as a friend and also…more?"

She swallowed and looked away. "Well, I guess we'll never know."

He paused, then shook his head. "No wonder you close a staggering seventy-five percent of your cases when most investigators are lucky to get thirty. You probably drive your suspects so insane, they'll confess to anything."

She was fairly certain that was not a compliment. "I'm good at what I do."

"Yes. Of that, there is no doubt. But how about other things outside the job?"

She was quiet a moment, trying to come to terms with what needed to be said. "There are some areas in my life that could use some work," she admitted. When he sent her a slow, knowing smile, she rolled her eyes and had to smile back. "I'm working on it," she said softly. "At my own pace."

"Nothing wrong with that."

# 4

THEIR PIZZA ARRIVED, and Ally dug in. After her long day, she felt like she was starving to death. She was halfway through her second piece before she realized Eddie was skimming the notes in her file and smiling.

"You've made a list of all the fire stations," he said. "Are we all under suspicion?"

When she didn't answer, he raised a brow, then kept reading. When he came to her list of suspects, he tossed back his head and laughed out loud. "Me? I'm your sole suspect?"

She lifted a shoulder.

Still smiling, his gaze ran slowly over her features. "Any time you want to search my person, you let me know." He turned a few pages. "A list of places that sell dirty wrapping paper. And a list of the adult novelty shops in the area. So what's the plan? You going to go storm them, gun blazing?"

"Give me my file."

"You are," he murmured, still grinning. "God, please let me watch."

She reached for the file but he slid it to his far side, making it so that she had to reach across him to get it. She was practically lying on his broad chest trying to grasp the papers when he let go of them and slid his hands up her arms.

Pleasure slammed into her and she went still. She was doing a pretty crappy job at that distance thing.

Eddie had gone still too, his long, leanly muscled body hard beneath hers. Slowly his gaze dropped to her mouth.

When she shivered, he leaned in to kiss her. And since she already knew he kissed like heaven on earth, her entire body shivered again in anticipation.

But instead of planting one on her, he reached past her for the sex manual, which fell open to a chapter entitled Sexual Fantasies.

"I probably could have written this chapter," he said.

Unsure if she was relieved or disappointed about the lack of a kiss, she sat back and grabbed another piece of pizza. "Let me guess. Your fantasies are about two women kissing, or two women naked, or better yet, two women kissing *and* naked."

His eyes dilated. "Not bad," he said, voice husky. "But mine tend to be more specific."

"Like?"

He arched his brow, silently asking if she really wanted to hear this, and her mouth promptly disconnected from her brain. "Tell me."

"You," he murmured. "My fantasy is you, in that little black dress and those do-me heels you wore at Thanksgiving."

She arched a brow, and he nodded.

She finally found her voice. "That actually seems relatively tame, me in the dress."

"With nothing beneath it except your gun."

She blinked.

He let out a low laugh. "Yeah, I get a lot of mileage out of reliving that scene at the Thanksgiving fire. Except in my fantasy, you're walking through my house instead of the warehouse. And you take me down instead of your perp, and then…"

His breathing roughened. "Sorry," he said with a shake of his head. "This is my favorite part. You slip out of the dress."

"Tell me I'm not really wearing just my gun beneath it."

"No." He smiled. "You're also wearing lipstick."

She shoved him to the far side of the booth and finished her pizza, trying not to think about why her belly was quivering. "I don't wear lipstick, I wear lip gloss."

"Even better."

"THANKS FOR the pizza," Ally murmured when they'd finished. "You can just take me back to my car."

Yes, Eddie got that loud and clear. She wanted him to go away. He'd always gotten that loud and clear from her. But apparently he'd been wrong, and that fascinated him. She fascinated him.

And she wanted him. The knowledge made him happier than he'd been in a long time, and he intended to return the favor.

When he drove past her office, heading into downtown, she sat up. "You missed my—"

"I know."

"Well, stop."

When he didn't, she sighed. "This is kidnapping. Unlawful restraint."

He slid her a look and a smile. "Going to cuff me?"

Her mouth tightened, and did so even more when five minutes later he pulled into the lot of Sally's Special XXX Toy Store.

"I'm not going to ask how you know where this place is," she said, the irony of the name of the shop not escaping her. Toy shop.

Toys.

That was where all the trouble had begun in the first place.

Eddie guided her inside, the file tucked beneath his arm. The place had black walls decorated with porn movie posters and neon signs that said things like Live Girls Nude and Hot Rod.

"Cute," she murmured beneath her breath.

He smiled. He loved how she was acting all tough and yet he had to practically push her through the store to the counter.

Sitting out on full display were a handful of vibrators, each bigger and more colorful than the last. Ally took a look at the largest one, which was a foot long and as wide around as her forearm, and tripped.

Eddie grinned and slipped an arm around her waist as he nodded to the guy behind the counter. The man was an indeterminable age, with a long straggly gray ponytail to his waist and a Grateful Dead T-shirt on his lean frame.

The clerk slid a look from Eddie to Ally, taking his time with her, before shifting back to Eddie again, a sly light in his eyes. "What can I do for you two this evening?"

Ally was looking at him long and hard. "Do I know you?"

The guy smiled wickedly. "Depends. You a regular customer?"

Eddie arched a brow at her, but Ally narrowed her eyes. "No," she said forcibly.

Eddie opened her file, revealing the picture of the massage oil. "You sell this here?" he asked the clerk.

"Nope. We have better than this."

Ally showed him the book. "How about this?"

The clerk flipped it open to the bookmarked page and grinned. "You having trouble with kissing?"

Ally appeared to grind her back teeth. "Just answer the question, please."

He scratched his head. "That's from Double D's Adult World on Ninth Street."

Allie had turned to walk away when he spoke again.

"But we sell the wrapping paper that you have in there."

Double D's Adult World was closed. Back in her office parking lot, Ally turned to Eddie. "Thanks for the backup."

"I'll watch your back anytime." He smiled. "Too bad Mr. Grateful Dead didn't have any way of knowing who'd recently purchased the wrapping paper. I thought you were going to pull your gun on him. Or maybe that was because he'd suggested you might be having trouble with kissing."

She got out and slammed the door, moving quickly toward her car, but he caught her just before she slid into her driver's seat. He wrapped one hand around her arm, the other going to her hip, gently pressing her against the side of her car. "Hey."

"Hey is for horses," she said.

With a slow smile, he leaned into her, his hard body coming into contact with hers, making her body instantly react. It knew, dammit, it knew the pleasure he could bring. Her nipples hardened against her top, and when his denim-clad leg slid between hers, she nearly moaned. Instead, she blew out a breath and met his amused gaze. "You're finding this whole thing funny, aren't you?"

"Some parts." He ran a finger over her temple, tucking a loose strand of hair behind her ear. "Not all."

She shivered but managed sarcasm. "Do tell."

"I like watching you run this like an official investigation. You're a deductive reasoner, a problem solver." He paused, his words raising goose bumps on her skin as he slid the same finger down her jaw, watching her carefully. "It makes me hot," he admitted. And then his lips grazed her earlobe, causing a full body shiver to wrack her.

She locked her knees. "You had your chance—"

His finger covered her lips. "Yeah, now that's the part I'm not amused by. I backed off, Ally, because I felt like I was pushing. I wanted you to want me." He stroked his thumb down her throat, his fingers stretching so that they just slid under the edge of her top, over her collarbone, coming to rest on the curve of her breast.

She felt a rush of lust.

"I want another chance at making you want me," he murmured, his fingers lightly teasing.

A shuddery sigh escaped her. "Th-that isn't the problem."

"Good." And then he slid his fingers into her hair and kissed her. The first touch of his tongue sent shockwaves of pleasure straight through her. Time seemed to stutter to a halt. Everything faded away except the feel of his hard muscles moving against her. And it wasn't just his muscles that were hard, she realized as his arousal nudged her leg. He held her, his hands gliding over her back, then beneath her top so that she could feel the warm roughness of his calloused palms.

"I missed this," he murmured, his breath hot and heavy on her neck, her throat, and she was shocked to find her own mouth at his shoulder, nipping at him. Her hands had made themselves at home beneath his shirt, as well, flat on his ridged abs, her fingers running over him like she was trying to read braille.

"Well that mystery is cleared up now," he murmured thickly, pressing his forehead to hers, clearly trying to draw air into his taxed lungs. "You definitely don't need that chapter on kissing."

"No?"

"No." He smiled. "You knock my socks off, Ally." His velvety green eyes met hers. "Come home with me. Let's try this again."

Her body perked up and sent a *please yes!* message to her brain. But she'd made a career out of caution, and exercised it now. "I don't want to revisit a mistake, Eddie."

She expected anger. Frustration at the very least. But he surprised her by pressing his mouth to her temple and gently stroking his hands over her back, soothing now instead of trying to ignite. "This thing with us isn't an investigation," he murmured. "It's not black and white, and it's not something you leave on your desk at the end of a hard day. It's real life, Ally."

"I know that."

"Then let go and give it a shot."

At her silence, he sighed and stepped back. "Think about it."

That, she could guarantee.

# 5

OVER THE NEXT SIX DAYS, Eddie put in four twenty-four hour shifts. At the end of the week, with only two weeks before Christmas, he staggered out of the station with Sam at his side.

"Shit," Sam murmured wearily, squinting at the winter sun as they stood and stared at the churning ocean. "I'm exhausted."

Eddie slid on his sunglasses and nodded, too tired to even agree verbally. He had a box of toys in his truck for Ally, but he needed a good solid eight hours prone on his bed before even thinking about being on his toes enough to face her.

The last time he'd seen her had been when he'd pressed her up against her car and kissed her like she was the very air he needed in his lungs. He'd asked her to give this, them, another shot.

And she'd vanished into the night, leaving him uncertain as to whether he'd just been denied, or if she was truly thinking about it.

He knew her. She was a careful, methodical, precise sort of woman who tended to live in a world where things could be solved by sheer tenacity and hard will. Once she'd made up her mind about something, it would take hell and high water to change it back. Unfortunately, he was fairly certain she'd made up her mind about him long ago.

"See you tomorrow night," Sam said, making Eddie realize that they were still just standing there in front of the beach, too tired to move.

"Tomorrow…"

"The game," Sam reminded him.

They played in a basketball league made up of cops, paramedics and firefighters, and they were in first place. "I'll be there."

"Bring your A game."

Eddie laughed. He *was* their A game and he knew it. He moved toward his truck and drove home on autopilot. Once there, he showered until he was out of hot water, dried off and fell into his big, comfy bed bare-ass naked.

He came awake to the sound of a doorbell, and lifted his head, blinking. It was six o'clock. His stomach said way past time to eat, pal. He rolled out of bed, grabbed up a pair of basketball shorts and headed to the front hall, thinking he felt a damn sight closer to human now.

He pulled open the door and blinked at Ally. She'd clearly come straight from work. Black trousers, pale blue fitted button-down shirt, dark sunglasses and an unreadable expression on her beautiful face. She held her *Secret Santa* file, clearing up any question as to whether she was there for business or pleasure.

"I'm sorry," she said immediately, her gaze dipping to take him in. "I woke you…up." She seemed to get snagged on the waistband of his shorts, so he looked down at himself.

They were low, probably indecently so because he hadn't bothered to tie them. He corrected that while she looked away. The tips of her ears reddened, and when she once again looked at him, her eyes didn't rise past his chest. "I didn't mean to, um." She rolled her bottom lip into her mouth. "I just wanted to…" She looked at his body, then tipped her head up and stared at the sky. "Toys. You hadn't brought the last shipment of toys so I went by the station. They told me you'd be here."

He leaned against the doorjamb. "Everything okay? You seem…flustered."

"You're not wearing a shirt. Or shoes." She swallowed hard and turned away. "And I'm intruding. I didn't mean to get you out of bed, I'm sorry, I gotta go, I—"

"Chicken," he said softly to her back. She straightened.

She whirled around. "What did you just call me?"

"You heard me."

She narrowed her eyes. "Well, that's just rude."

Pushing away from the doorjamb, he took the two steps down to her and pulled off her sunglasses. "There. That's a little better," he murmured. "Now look me in the eyes and tell me you feel nothing for me. That you're perfectly willing to just walk away and never know."

"Know what?" she whispered.

"What happens next."

She just stared at him, a mixture of yearning and confusion chasing each other across her pretty face, and he took mercy on her. "If I put on a shirt, will you be able to string together a full sentence?"

She went beet red, then covered her cheeks. After a moment, she let out a jerky nod. "Maybe."

He laughed, took her hand, and pulled her into his house. "Be right back." Moving into his bedroom, he grabbed a T-shirt, then shrugged into it before joining her. She'd waited for him in the living room and was standing next to the box of toys on his coffee table.

She didn't look at him as he came back into the room, but her ears were no long flaming. "I figured I'd come to you this time," she said. "We could paw through the box right here on your turf."

"In order to scratch me off your list of suspects once and for all, right?"

She was silent so long, he didn't expect an answer. But then she lifted her head and met his gaze straight on. "Actually, I don't think it's you."

He opened his mouth, then shut it again. "Thanks," he finally said as she lifted a shiny silver-wrapped, naked Santa covered package the size of a DVD. "Damn," she whispered.

"You have got to be kidding." Eddie strode over to her just as she pulled off the paper.

A little squeak escaped her as she looked at the porno flick. He took it from her. *"Here Cums Santa Claus,"* he read. "Interesting." He sank to the couch, opened his laptop and stuck the DVD in.

Ally stared at him. "What are you doing?"

"Checking out the evidence."

"Oh my God." She sounded like she couldn't decide whether she should be horrified or morbidly curious as his DVD player booted up the disk and went to the menu.

Eddie hit Play, and almost immediately, in tune to some really badly orchestrated music, two stacked women walked into an office wearing red, fur-lined bikinis. They were arguing over who was going to shack up with the Jolly Old Elf this year, and then a guy in red swim trunks and a Santa hat strolled in and declared that whoever gave him the best blow job could help him ensure quality control over the "toys."

Ally sank to the couch beside Eddie as if her knees had given out.

"Should we see who wins?" he asked her.

Before she could answer, both women were on their knees, peeling back Santa's suit, freeing his—

"Oh my God," Ally said again. There were two spots of high color on her cheeks, her eyes were glossy, her mouth open. If he wasn't mistaken, she was definitely leaning more toward being morbidly curious than horrified.

And maybe even a little turned on.

They watched for a moment, but when "Santa" started barking like a dog, Eddie hit Stop.

Slowly Ally turned to him. "Men really like that?"

Was she referring to the blow job or the two women at the same time thing? "Some," he said carefully.

She chewed on that for a minute. "I just don't get the whole making animal noises," she finally said, causing him to choke out a laugh and sling an arm around her, tugging her in for a hug. God, she was something.

"What do you think these presents mean?" she asked him.

He'd been trying to figure that out himself. "Maybe someone's just messing with you. Have you tried to link these pranks with one of your cases?"

"Yes." She opened her file to a page where she'd documented all her ongoing cases, and any possible links she'd found. She'd listed two, both extremely long shots according to her. Thanks to her very new arson investigative/criminal profiling software, she'd been able to put their chances at being connected at less than five percent.

He flipped the pages to see what else she had and at the very back, found something that caught his attention.

His name.

Then hers.

And then a little penciled in note that said 'also less than five percent'. He looked at her.

"It's our chances at being connected. To each other," she clarified.

"Less than five percent? Really?"

"I don't like getting hurt."

"Ally." He shook his head. "I never meant to hurt you the first time."

She nodded, chewed on her lips, and then let out a low breath. "I know that now."

He entwined their fingers together and looked at her for a long moment. "You're still thinking?"

"Yes." She nodded, but her eyes were very solemn. "But

less than five percent, Eddie? Those are some pretty rough odds."

Yeah, they were. "But it's better than zero." And when she just stared at him, he smiled. "And it's not impossible."

# 6

NOT IMPOSSIBLE.

Ally got to her feet. "I need to go." She moved to the door, put her hand on the handle, then hesitated. She didn't know why, or maybe she did.

Eddie's hands settled on her hips, and he turned her to face him.

She hadn't even heard him move, but here he was, standing a breath away, six feet plus of solid, gorgeous, hard muscle. "You know what people, women, say about you?" she murmured, heart pounding as he cupped her face and slowly shook his head.

"They say that you're fun." She gave him a little smile, which was hard to do with her heart in her throat. "That you're exciting and adventurous. I think I pulled away because I was afraid. I'm a workaholic," she said, trying to explain to him, to her. "I'm *not* all that fun or exciting. I guess I can't imagine what there is about me that would keep your interest."

"Are you kidding me?" His thumbs stroking her jaw. "You're the smartest woman I know. Do you have any idea what a turn-on that is? You're loyal and warm, and your heart…" He slowly shook his head, his emotions so visible, it shocked her.

Softened her.

Tilting her chin, he kissed her, sweet and soft and

romantic. "Your heart is real. Genuine," he whispered against her lips. "It makes mine turn over in my chest, Ally."

She dragged in a deep breath, shocked at the level of his honesty. *Distance* had been her word of the month, but he so effortlessly melted away her resistance. All of it. Even knowing she was going to get hurt couldn't seem to stop her from wanting him.

And she did want him.

She always had.

His arms tightened and he kissed her again, not so sweet this time, not so soft. The connection started a slow burn, and when they finally came up for air, he looked into her eyes so fiercely she squirmed, unnerved at letting him see so much.

"And as for the fun and exciting," he said softly. "Do you know anyone else getting X-rated presents? Because I sure as hell don't."

She opened her mouth and he took full advantage of that, pinning her back against the door, kissing her again until she couldn't remember what she'd been about to say.

"What do I have to do?" His mouth was at her ear, his breath hot against her skin. "To prove myself."

"Prove yourself?"

"You don't believe I want you. I want you, Ally," he murmured, spreading hot, open-mouthed kisses along her jaw, down her throat. "So damn much. Christ, if I wanted you any more than I already do, we'd be going up in flames right about now."

"I do feel a little like I'm on fire…"

Laughing softly, he looked into her eyes, his hard body holding hers, searching. "Does that mean you want me back?"

"More than my next breath," she admitted.

With a smile that curled her toes, he took her hand, pulling her down a hall to what was clearly his bedroom. She stared at the huge bed, pictured them there naked and sweaty, and she nearly collapsed.

"Ally."

"Yeah?" She was still staring at the bed.

With a finger beneath her chin, he turned her face to his. His eyes were hot, God so hot, and also so very solemn. "Second thoughts?"

She swallowed. "I can't remember my first thoughts, much less second ones…"

He didn't budge, not to kiss her, and not to get them naked and sweaty, which meant she was going to have to say it. "No," she whispered. "No second thoughts. Well, except that I don't think we're going to need the oil, the book or the DVD. But a condom might come in handy."

He smiled with more than a little relief and a whole lot of wicked intent as he pulled a strip of condoms from his nightstand.

Five. Five just might be enough, she thought. Then she shocked them both by fisting her hands in his hair and pulling his mouth to hers, sinking her teeth into his lower lip before sucking his tongue into her mouth.

He groaned and reached for her, his hands at her shirt, unbuttoning it, tugging it down her arms, tossing it to a chair behind him as he reached for the button on her pants.

Before she could draw in her next breath, she stood there in nothing but her bra and panties. He let out a rough appreciative sound at the sight of her, one hand cupping a breast, his thumb strumming her nipple, the other hand cupping one butt cheek, the tips of his fingers brushing the damn satin between her legs.

"Wait," she gasped. "You. Now you," she demanded.

He reached back, grabbed a fistful of his shirt and yanked it off over his head while she tugged down his basketball shorts.

He was naked, gloriously hard and naked and perfect except for the long gash and bruise on his thigh that was healing nicely. She said the first thing that came to mind. "You could have starred in that DVD."

With a quick grin, he slid off her bra, then nudged her down to sit on the bed as he dropped to his knees before her. With a hand on either side of her hips, he leaned over her, his mouth going to a breast. He whispered a kiss over her, lightly rubbing his rough jaw against the curve.

Again she fisted her hands in his hair, helplessly holding on as he brushed another kiss over her, his hands gliding down her ribs, her hips, along the edge of her panties.

And then a calloused finger traced over the very core of her.

Her head fell back, her lips parted. She could hardly breathe for wanting his mouth on her breasts, his fingers inside her. "Eddie—"

"You're so beautiful," he murmured, and finally pulled her nipple into his mouth, sucking it between his tongue and the roof of his mouth just as a finger glided against her wet flesh, pressing and stroking in exactly the right rhythm to make her cry out and arch her hips.

"And so hot, Ally." His mouth moved down her belly, kissing first one hip, then other, before sliding her panties down her legs. When his hands went to her thighs and spread them, she tried to speak but her words were unintelligible. He didn't ask her to repeat them.

He simply put his fingers to work.

She came like that, and then again when he leaned in to add his tongue and teeth to the mix. She nearly burst for a third time when he crawled up her body and slid inside her, but then she'd heard him groan low and rough in her ear that he was going to come.

When he did, when he thrust into her hard and let go, his face a mask of exquisite pleasure as he shuddered, she lost it.

Completely.

And then they spent the next deliciously long dark hours finding it again….

EDDIE WOKE UP with the sun shining in his face and a light, odd, sort of floaty feeling deep in his gut—which, if he remembered correctly, signified happiness. He had a warm body pressed to his side, her arm and leg thrown over him, her cheek on his chest.

Last night had been…

Off the charts.

He felt the grin split his face, and before he even opened his eyes, he rolled Ally to her back and pressed her into the mattress. How long had he been wanting this? Too goddamn long, and now here she was, wearing nothing but his sheet and looking gorgeously rumpled and sated. "This," he murmured, his hands sliding down to squeeze her sweet ass, rocking her into him. "This is the only way to wake up."

She hummed an agreement. "You've been 'up' for a few minutes now."

"Have I?" Bending his head, he nibbled his way along her shoulder, up her throat… "Any ideas on what to do about it?"

"Are you kidding? We went through my entire repertoire of ideas about five hours ago."

"I'm sure we can come up with something."

"Well, there is one condom left…"

Oh yeah. He shifted, the weight of his body driving her deeper into the mattress, making her moan at the feel of him on top of her as she opened her legs, welcoming him.

Her hands caressed his face, his shoulders, down his back and then to his ass, digging in with her fingers as she shivered in anticipation. It seemed that Investigator Ally wanted him to hurry.

And he aimed to oblige.

But he wanted to taste her again first. Sliding down her

body, he put his hands on her thighs, keeping contact with her as he lifted her up to his mouth. When he gently sucked her in, her body bowed, her hands fisting in the sheets as she gasped his name.

God, he loved her like this. He wasn't sure he could ever get enough. When she shattered, he crawled up her body, twined their hands together beside her head and drove into her with one fierce thrust. Her hips rocked to meet his, setting a rhythm as they stared at each other. Her legs were high around his waist, gripping him as tight as he gripped her. They were hand to hand, eyes locked as they shattered together this time.

It was the most erotic, sensual experience of his life.

Moments or years later, they lay there flat on their backs, still gasping for air.

"That was…" Her words trailed off.

"Yeah," was all he could manage to say. "It was."

After another few moments, he felt her shift. He opened his eyes and looked at her.

"Maybe," she said very seriously. "Maybe it's just that we're addicted to sex."

He grinned. "Complaints?"

"Not a single one."

That had him laughing out loud. "Good," he finally said, and buried his face in her hair. "God, I love your scent."

"I'm not wearing anything."

"I know." He kissed the spot beneath her ear, the one that he'd discovered made her hum with pleasure, and smiled when she shivered.

"I would have thought you'd have had your fill of me by now," she murmured.

She had no idea. No idea that he was falling, and falling hard. He stroked a hand down her side, then back up again, lightly skimming his knuckles over a nipple, watching it pucker for him. "I don't think that's possible," he said a little hoarsely.

"We went all night—" She gasped as he bent his head and ran his tongue over her nipple. "In the shower, on the kitchen counter—" She stopped to moan as he lightly blew over the spot he'd just licked.

"And the hallway floor," he reminded her.

That one had been her doing. But he'd enjoyed every single screaming minute of it.

Cupping her face, he lifted his head and met her eyes. "I wasn't sure I'd find you here this morning. I'm glad you stayed."

"I tried to leave at dawn. You…"

Stroking her hair out of her eyes, he smiled. "I what?"

"You…dissuaded me."

"Did I?"

"You know very well you did. You said there were still a few spots on my body that you hadn't tasted yet, and then you…" She squirmed.

"What?" he murmured, as turned on now as he'd been last night.

"You put your mouth on me."

His favorite part. "You taste so good, Ally."

She closed her eyes. "You have this way, you know. Of making me feel…"

He waited for her to finish that thought. He made her feel what exactly? But when she remained quiet, he realized that there was no qualifier on the end of her sentence. He made her feel.

Period.

And his heart caught, hard. But when he bent to kiss her, she slapped a hand to his chest. "We have work," she said. "We have to get up and go collect the rest of the toys. Together."

"Aw, how sweet." He kissed one corner of her mouth, then the other. "You want to spend time with me." He smiled when she scowled, because that hadn't been what she meant and he knew it. She still didn't fully trust him. That was okay, they'd work on it.

Her stomach growled. "Great. I probably have mascara all over my face, a major case of bed head, and now you know how loudly my stomach can growl."

"I don't see any mascara, or bed head. Although…" He brushed his fingers over the silky strands. "It definitely has a 'just been thoroughly ravished' look to it." He grinned when she groaned. "And my stomach can outdo yours any day of the week, trust me. Come on, I'll feed you."

"Shower first."

"Shower first, then."

With that, he rolled out of bed and yanked the sheet off her.

She squeaked, then sat up and eyed his hard-on. "Again?" she asked as he lifted her into his arms.

She was trying to sound resigned, but he could hear the low tremor of excitement in her voice she couldn't hide.

It cracked him up. He stopped for a long, slow kiss that had her panting and clinging to his lips. He pulled back just enough to say, "And you think *I'm* the addict."

## 7

THEY DIDN'T GET LUCKY in the shower. In fact, he let her go first. Ally didn't know whether to be disappointed or relieved that he wouldn't be once again effortlessly pulling a shocking amount of desire, passion and need out of her, not to mention the emotions.

God, the emotions.

She'd had no idea.

None.

But being with the *right* guy, having him touching her the right way, making her feel…

*Right.*

After her shower, he fed her. He stood in his kitchen in worn jeans, a faded firefighter T-shirt, and a day's growth of beard shadowing his jaw, and made her an omelet and toast, looking sexy as hell while he did it.

In the light of day it hit her just how hot he was, how virile and potent his sheer presence was.

And he was completely unaware of it.

When he caught her staring at him, his usual easy smile was replaced with something far more devastating—a deep, almost fierce intensity.

"What?" she whispered, but he shook his head, shrugged it off, and then he pulled her out of her chair and kissed her until neither of them could think. After they'd eaten, he asked her about her plan for the day.

Her plan.

He hadn't tried to push his own agenda on her, hadn't tried to take over, hadn't done anything but show her in every move, every step, every word he uttered that he completely and totally respected her job and her ability to do it.

Did he have any idea how attractive that was? How he made her want things she'd already decided weren't in the cards for her?

"So where to?" he repeated quietly, making her realize she'd been staring at him stupidly for God knew how long.

"Let's go pick up toys at the stations," she said.

"I like the 'let's.'"

That afternoon, he drove her to the first of the three fire stations in town. There was half a box of toys there, and Eddie handed them to her one by one.

No surprises in the bottom.

Same thing at the second fire station.

At the third, Eddie's own firehouse, the stack of gifts was bigger. Once again they went through their routine, Eddie pulling out each toy one by one, until he stopped handing them over to her.

"That's it?" she asked, holding her breath, wanting to be relieved, searching his face for a clue.

She found it in the slight tightening of his mouth.

He lifted a package wrapped in shiny gold, with the ever-present naked Santas all over it. This box was about a foot long, only a few inches wide, and she stared at it like it was a spitting cobra. "Damn."

He took her out to his truck to pull off the paper. Ally felt her mouth open and then close and then open again. She was impersonating a goldfish.

A struck-dumb goldfish.

Eddie took the foot-long vibrator from her hands. "Interesting color."

It was as purple as Barney the Dinosaur. "What the hell am I supposed to do with this?" she finally murmured.

"Spend another night with me and I'll show you."

Her insides quivered, her body recognizing the truth of his statement. She stared at him, trying to frown but her damn nipples went hard. "You'd…you want to…with this."

His smile was downright wicked. "I've never been much for toys, but I know how thorough you can be. If you wanted to check this out, I'd feel obligated to assist. Or at the very least, watch."

"It's evidence." But she looked at the thing again with just enough speculation to make him laugh. God, she loved his laugh. Shoving him, she looked at the box. "Hey, look. There's a store tag here." It was for a porn shop in the next town over, one they hadn't visited.

Half an hour later, they were on their way there, Eddie driving with easy, calm efficiency. He still wore those old jeans and T-shirt, dark glasses over his eyes now. He hadn't shaved, and she thought of how that rough jaw would feel between her thighs tonight. Then she realized she had no idea *if* she was going to see him tonight.

Or the next night.

She had no claim on him. None. She'd slept with him, period. And though she didn't regret it, not a single moment, she also knew that things were different than before. Months ago, her heart hadn't been fully engaged. Now it definitely was.

As for his heart, she had no idea. Men didn't work the same way women did. They could get naked and not get attached.

Eddie slid her a glance. "You okay?"

"I am." Let it go, please let it go…

"Looks like you're deep in thought."

She opened her mouth, but in the end, she didn't say anything.

He looked as if he wanted to push the issue, but they were already at the porn shop. The door was locked. Looking at the sign, they realized the store didn't open for another fifteen minutes. They waited at Eddie's truck, where he tugged her to him. "Hey."

"Hey."

He smiled, but when she didn't, he lifted his sunglasses to the top of his head. "Want to tell me those deep thoughts now?"

"No."

He studied her a moment, then pressed her back against the door. "You remember when I was telling you all the things I liked about you? That you're smart as hell, and gorgeous, and you make me want things that I've never wanted before?"

She didn't remember that last part, no. Her breath caught, because in spite of herself, she liked the sound of it.

"I also like your honesty," he said quietly, nudging her face up to his. "It's such an innate part of you. If you feel something, if you think something, you say it. No hidden meanings, no subterfuge. I love that." He lifted her hand to his mouth and kissed her palm. "So employ that honesty with me now, Ally, and tell me what's on your mind. Just say it."

She stared into his deep green eyes and imagined herself, telling him that she suddenly had all these feelings for him, feelings that were new and terrifying... She opened her mouth to say something, then frowned at the sight of the guy standing in front of the porn shop, unlocking the door. "Store's opening."

The clerk wasn't wearing a Grateful Dead T-shirt, or even a long gray ponytail, but somehow she knew. Dammit, she *knew* it was the same guy. In a beat, she was out of Eddie's arms. "Excuse me," she said to the clerk.

He turned and swore roughly. "What, do you never give up?"

"It *is* you," she breathed, and then it hit her. He was also the "toy director" she'd met at the Thanksgiving fire. "Okay, I want to know who you are, what you're doing working at three different porn shops, and why you're stalking me. And I want to know *right now.*"

"Christ you are a pain in the ass. You're like a freaking bulldog. Can't you just accept that there are some things in life that don't need a full-blown investigation?"

"Your name," she said, voice hard.

He sighed. "Damon Claus."

"And?"

He rolled his eyes. "And what? You going to shoot me if I don't talk? In case you haven't noticed, it's Christmas, lady. You don't shoot people this time of year, it's just not done."

She put her hand on the gun at her hip. "Try me."

He shook his head and looked over at Eddie. "You might want to rethink this one, she's nuts."

Eddie shifted closer, big and tall and menacingly calm, clearly ready to step in if required.

"Start talking," Ally demanded of Damon.

He caved with a tight little smile. "You want the full story? Fine. I'm Santa Claus's brother and—"

"Try again," Ally said.

"Yeah, yeah, you don't believe me."

"Sure, I believe you. You're Santa's brother. And I'm the Tooth Fairy." She pulled out her cell phone and tossed it to Eddie. "Be ready to call for backup."

Damon shook his head. "Trust me, I wish I didn't have to believe me, either. But Santa's pissing me off with all the freaking jolly, okay? So I've made it my—let's call it my mission in life, to stomp on the good cheer whenever possible."

Clearly the guy needed psychiatric care. "And?"

"Well you're going to be spreading a lot of good tidings with that toy drive. I just thought if I distracted you…" Here he paused to waggle his eyebrows between her and Eddie suggestively. "Then maybe you'd screw up."

"I don't get distracted," Ally said.

"Really." Damon gestured toward her neck with his chin. "So I suppose that isn't a hickey there, and you didn't get laid last night."

When Ally slapped her hand to her neck and narrowed her eyes at him, he just smiled. "Look, unless you're going to arrest me, you'll need to move along now and let me get to my job. I live to sell butt plugs and lube."

Ally stared at him, fighting the very unprofessional urge to kick his ass, or at the very least arrest him. But for what? Gifting her with sex toys?

Damon must have seen the resignation in her gaze because he laughed, winked at her, then slipped like smoke into the shop.

In disbelief, Ally turned to Eddie. A smile crossed his face and he shook his head.

"What?" she asked, a little defensively.

"Your interviewing skills turn me on."

"Everything turns you on."

"Want to interrogate me?"

Some of the tension left her and she laughed before she could help herself. "You need help."

"Seriously. I'll even let you use the cuffs."

# 8

EDDIE TOOK ALLY back to his house. He'd hoped to help her work off the adrenaline clearly humming through her, but she grabbed her purse and would have hopped out of his truck and into her car with nothing but a quietly murmured "bye" if he hadn't managed to catch her by the back of her shirt.

"I've got to go, Eddie."

"In a minute." Maybe. He looked into her eyes. "We were interrupted before, when you were about to tell me something important."

"How do you know it was important?"

Her eyes were filled with a lot of things. Hell, that was no surprise, she had a lot going on. But behind all of it was a hint of panic, and something even bigger.

She needed to run.

He got that. God, he did. She needed to run because she had come to realize just how far in she was. Except surely she also realized she was in too far to retreat now, that they both were.

Just as she had to realize something else, something even more devastating.

What they shared was more than simple attraction. He was completely head over heels in love with her, and had been this whole time. "I just know," he said very quietly.

"ESP?" She let out a forced laugh. "You think you can read my mind?"

"And your heart, when you wear it on your sleeve." When she tried to jerk free, he gently took her arms and hauled her into his lap. "Stop," he said softly as she fought him.

She went still for a beat, then sagged against him, pressing her face to his throat as her arms slid up his chest. "I'm not sure where we were exactly."

"Liar. You always know where you are."

She let out a small sound that might have been agreement.

"Here. I'll go first," he said, wrapping his fingers in her hair, then gently tugging until she looked at him. "We've been seeing each other because of the toy drive."

She slowly nodded. "Yes. Sorry if that's been a trial for you." She slipped off his lap and back into her seat.

"That's not what I meant, Ally."

She hugged herself and looked out the window. "Listen, you don't have to do this—"

"Yes, I do. I want you to know I'm not going to make the same mistake I made last time. I'm not going to walk away. Not now that I know what we have."

"And what's that?"

"Affection, for starters. Heat, in spades. And the chemistry? Off the charts." He wished she'd look at him. "And…"

"What?" she breathed, finally turning her eyes to his.

"A future. If you'll let it happen. I'm falling in love with you, Ally."

All the color drained from her face. "You…you're…" She made a noise of distress and pressed a hand to her heart.

"Breathe," he murmured, reaching for her.

She gulped in a breath and dropped her head to his chest. "Just give me a minute."

He shook his head and let out a small smile. "You face badass arsonists and creepy stalkers on a daily basis. You carry a gun and know how to take down a guy twice your size. Yet you're afraid of a little emotion."

"Yeah, well, they didn't teach this in Fire Science. And there's nothing little about this emotion."

"Ally—"

She lifted her head. "I'm sorry, but at least you now know just how dysfunctional I am."

"Dysfunctional, or scared?"

"Fine. Terrified." She reached for the door handle. "I have a meeting."

"How about dinner?"

"I'll be working late."

He looked into her face for a long moment. "You know where I live. Show up if you want to finish this, even if it's late." He leaned in and kissed her.

She held herself still for one beat, then let out a sexy little murmur and kissed him back. When he lifted his mouth from hers a few minutes later, her eyes were glazed over and she was struggling for breath.

He cupped her face and kissed her one more time. He couldn't help himself. "I love you, Ally." And with that, he leaned across her, opened the door and gently nudged her out.

He watched her drive away, catching her taking a bewildered, WTF peek at him in her rearview mirror. She was confused and turned on and unsure, all things he could identify with.

He only hoped she figured out she was also in love.

ALLY DROVE to work on auto-pilot, then walked slowly into the building, knees wobbling, heart pounding, sweating in uncomfortable places.

Cherry handed her a stack of messages. A few co-workers came out of their office to chat, her boss stuck his head out to bark that she was late for her meeting.

After the meeting, she walked out and couldn't have repeated a single thing that had transpired in that conference room.

Because Eddie…loved her.

Loved.

Her.

Clearly he was as delusional as Damon Claus, because something between the two of them could never work. He was too easygoing, too laid-back, too…

Perfect.

She'd drive him out of his ever-loving mind with her carefulness, her obsession for details, her need to work 24/7. He'd be running for the hills in no time.

Except he seemed to like her just the way she was. He'd only backed off before because she'd seemed disinterested. And as for the rest, he'd never hinted at wanting to change her, mold her, or soften her in any way. In fact, he liked her work style. He seemed to like most everything about her.

Except her ability to tell him what she felt.

Yeah, that was a problem for him. She couldn't blame him there. Especially when she did know. She'd always known. He was right. She'd held back because of fear, which was inexcusable really.

She didn't do fear. At least not in her job. In her job, she was fearless, facing everything straight on.

But…

But in her life, she was anything but fearless.

It was a hell of a time to realize that. She opened the *Secret Santa* file, went straight to the back and looked at the odds she'd come up with for her and Eddie.

Five percent was too low, she knew that now. So she erased the number and put in a different one.

And then hoped she could make true.

EDDIE ORDERED pizza and beer, then bribed Sam over to help him add some patio stones to the backyard. They devoured the pizza and were still laying the stones when a knock came at the door.

"It's probably Sara," Sam said, groaning as he got off his knees. "She said she might come by with dessert. I'll get her."

Eddie set another stone before Sam came back with a funny look on his face. "Well?" Eddie asked. "Did she bring dessert?"

"Yeah, man. I think so." Then Sam did the oddest thing. He grinned broadly, slapped Eddie on the shoulder, grabbed his keys, and headed out. "Set your alarm. We have an eight o'clock morning shift, and I have a feeling it's going to be a late one for ya."

And then, still chortling, he was gone.

What the hell? Eddie straightened, stretched his aching back and moved into the living room, then stopped short.

Ally stood there, wearing a hot little black dress, emphasis on the little, and four inch heels, showing a lot of skin and nerves. He just about staggered. He put a hand to his heart, checking to see if it had stopped. Because it sure looked as if he'd died and gone to heaven.

"Hey," she said softly, a little uncertain. "You said late was okay, so…"

Because his voice suddenly failed him, he nodded.

She took a deep breath, then reached down and did something that started his heart again, as if he'd been jolted with 220 volts. She ran her hands up her right thigh, bringing up the already heart-stopping hem of the dress even farther, revealing…ah, Christ…a holster.

She was armed.

"I'm going to have to ask you to turn away from me," she said in a soft but authoritative voice. "Spread 'em, and place your hands on the wall."

His jaw hit the floor.

"I only want to ask you a few questions, and as long as you cooperate, I won't have to get rough."

Already hard as a rock, he turned to the wall, put his hands flat on the plaster texture. He felt her come up behind him and put her hands on his hips. Her breasts brushed his back and he closed his eyes, loving the feel of her.

"Did you mean it?" she whispered against the nape of his neck, leaving her lips on him, slowly gliding them back and forth across his heated flesh as her fingers slid beneath the hem of his T-shirt.

"I meant it," he said gruffly. "I love you, Ally."

He could hear her breathing, a little too quickly, and he felt as if he could feel her heart pounding through her chest and into his back.

"What were your plans?" She ran her fingers over his abs, which appeared to make her breathe even faster. "Eddie?"

He was having trouble thinking. "Plans?"

"With me," she clarified.

"I'm going to lick every inch of you until you're screaming my name." He set his forehead to the wall. She was no longer the only one panting for air. "And then I'm going to—"

"No." She pressed her lips to his shoulder and let out a shaky laugh. "I meant with us. After…this."

He tried to turn to face her, but she tightened her grip on him, silently asking him to stay still.

Her fingers drifted up and down his abs and chest beneath his shirt, over his nipples, then down, playing with the buttons on his Levi's, making him groan out her name. "My plans are to love you for as long as you'll let me," he managed to say, his voice low and raspy even to his own ears. When she lightly stroked a finger over his button-fly, his knees nearly buckled. "I want to be with you," he said. "See where this goes."

Needing to see her reaction, he turned to face her.

She stared at him, then once again reached beneath her dress. She removed the holster and set it aside. Then in one fluid motion, she pulled the dress off, leaving her in nothing but—

"Just the lip gloss."

His greatest fantasy.

She drew a shaky breath. "I love you back, Eddie. And I want to be with you. To see where this thing goes. But I hope to God it's going to the bedroom at the moment. I wasn't sure because you never did finish telling me about your fantasy…"

He felt the wide grin split his face just as love for her split his heart. In one step, he had her against him, in his arms. "*You're* the rest of my fantasy," he told her. "Just you."

To my novella mates, Vicki Lewis Thompson
and Jill Shalvis.

You girls rock.

# SNUG IN HIS BED
## Rhonda Nelson

# 1

VIV FOSTER, LAMENTABLY, had always had a talent for getting into trouble.

In grade school she'd spent more time in the corner than at her desk, usually for talking or for being out of her seat. Or for accidentally setting a small fire with her magnifying glass. She winced. That little experiment had been a trifle too successful.

Her high school career had been punctuated with glaring stares from exasperated teachers and the occasional trip to detention, but nothing too extraordinarily terrible.

Though she'd made more than a few visits to the principal's office, she'd never been expelled. Throughout college and into her adult years, she'd always managed to hold on to her tongue—or her temper, whichever the case may be—and straddle that fine line between civilized, mature woman and out-of-control, screaming harpy.

Unfortunately, she'd tripped over the line recently and had landed herself in the one place she never expected to be.

*Court.*

"I still can't believe you attacked Santa Claus," Minna Waverly, her attorney and long-time friend leaned over and said as they stood before the judge.

Viv smothered an irritated sigh. "Oh, for heaven's sake, I didn't attack Santa Claus. I cold-cocked a mall Santa for copping a feel. There's a difference."

And the arrogant bastard had it coming, if you asked her.

Honestly, the guy had been giving her The Stare for the past week, whistling and making inappropriate little comments and gestures every time she'd had the misfortune cross his path.

And the hell of it was, she'd purposely *avoided* it.

Last week she'd seen him coming toward her down the main mall avenue and she'd actually made an abrupt detour through one of the larger department stores with an exit to the parking lot—acres of freezing asphalt away from where she'd left her bloody car—in order to miss him.

To her utter shock and irritation, he'd been leaning against the very door she'd planned to go through, though how he'd gotten there ahead of her was a total mystery.

Damned Christmas season, Viv thought. If she hadn't been so strapped for cash, she wouldn't have taken a second job as an "elf" at the gift wrapping station. But her brood of nieces and nephews, not to mention all of her other relatives, expected a gift come Christmas Eve. And she had too much pride to say she couldn't afford it this year, and enough sense to avoid racking up a lot of debt on her for-emergencies-only credit card. She'd spent too many years wearing hand-me-down clothes and eating noodles to ever forget the value of a dollar.

Regardless of all the hype, there was no such thing as a *free* ride.

Furthermore, she was absolutely determined to give herself a gift this Christmas that had been two years in the making—a trip to London. A little thrill whipped through her at the thought. Clotted cream and scones, Big Ben and the Thames. She loved Brit-coms and was the ultimate Anglophile. She desperately wanted to go.

Her Web-design business was growing steadily thanks to happy clients and word-of-mouth advertising. But like a lot of other businesses not directly related to retail, it tended to take a hit during the holidays. Like her, too many people were buckling down to cover the looming expense of Christmas and other things—like a new site or redesign—were getting pushed to a later date.

Come February, she'd have more business than she could handle. Until then, she'd simply have to make do. And at the moment, making do meant wrapping gifts in the Wrap It Up kiosk in Jackson, Mississippi's Magnolia Blossom Mall.

She rolled her eyes and glared at the attorney who represented Mr. Touchy-Feely—he couldn't be bothered to show up himself—and silently wished she could avoid Christmas altogether. While most other people carried around happy snow globe memories of their childhood Christmases, Viv's had been radically different.

The year she'd turned eight, her father had decided that Christmas morning was the best time to pack up and leave his family. Through a child's eyes, all Viv had seen were her parents arguing and her father going away as a result.

Naturally, she'd blamed her mother.

Now that she was an adult, she could see things more clearly. Looking back on that Christmas morning she remembered her mother helping her set up her Easy Bake Oven, even though her husband had just left her for another woman. Viv was in complete awe of her mom. She'd put her children first and her own heartbreak second and had tried to make things as normal as possible. That took a strength of character Viv wasn't altogether certain she possessed.

Three years later she'd seen her father in a toy store with a toddler in tow, one who was the spitting image of her dad. It's funny the things you notice, Viv thought now. The boy had been wearing a denim conductor's hat and his overall straps had been twisted. They'd been picking out a new train set, happy and oblivious to her stunned stare. Too much pride and too little courage had prevented her from approaching the pair, but she often wondered about that little boy. Her baby brother, she thought with a pang of regret. She'd wanted to know that little boy and felt like a part of her life was incomplete because she didn't.

Though she imagined her mother was aware of her father's new family, Viv had never mentioned seeing them. Why? She wasn't altogether certain. In the days immediately following the incident, she'd come close to saying something to her older sister, but for reasons she couldn't quite explain, she'd kept it to herself.

While she had grieved the loss of her father who'd literally vanished from their lives that Christmas morning, she had to admit that never knowing that little boy seemed like the greater tragedy.

"All right. Let's get this over with," the judge intoned in a boring drawl from the bench. "My lunch is getting cold." He perused the documents in front of him. "Assault, eh?"

He smirked, and Viv noticed there was something strangely familiar about him. A prickle of unease nicked her heart. She frowned and studied him more closely. Impossibly, he bore a marked resemblance to Damon Claus, the very mall Santa who had landed her in this unfortunate predicament. She blinked, equally stunned and unsure.

He smiled and winked at her.

Viv gasped and nudged Minna. *Holy shit.* "Minna, that's *him*," she hissed frantically, panic and disbelief kicking her heart rate into stroke level. But how could— This wasn't possible— *Oh, Lord. She was doomed.* She'd end up in jail in one of those ghastly orange jumpsuits, the reluctant love interest of a big girl named Pansy. She shuddered, horrified.

"Him, who?" Minna asked, seemingly confused.

"Him, as in *the mall Santa*," Viv told her, a cold sweat breaking out across her shoulders.

Minna's eyes widened. "You're joking."

Viv knew the vein in her forehead was throbbing. "Do I *look* like I'm joking?"

"It can't be him," her friend argued. She glanced at the judge and a speculative gleam entered her gaze. "Though I have to admit I've never seen this guy before."

Oh, Lord help her. Her knees went weak. "What am I going to do?"

"It's not him," Minna insisted. "You assaulted Damon Claus. This is Judge Nick Moroz. He's new," she conceded. "But he can't be both men."

It was a sound argument, but Viv couldn't shake the sensation that the two men were actually one in the same. Their striking physical appearance aside, they both had the same grin, a bit wicked and disconcertingly attractive.

Managing to appear both uninterested and amused, Judge Moroz asked for her plea.

"Not guilty," Minna said with a brisk nod.

He quirked an indolent brow. "Really? I've got a sworn statement here from a Mr. Jimmy Hall, head of mall security, who says he personally witnessed the attack on Mr. Claus."

*Attack?* They made her sound like a mad woman. "What Mr. Hall *didn't* witness was Mr. Claus grabbing my ass," Viv said, her temper flaring. Honestly, this was all such an utter joke.

Minna grabbed her arm and squeezed a warning. "What my client means to say is that she was provoked, your honor. Mr. Claus sexually harassed her."

He propped his chin into his hand and gave Viv another one of those inane smiles. "Really? Did she file a complaint?"

"No, sir," Minna replied, a bit uncomfortably. "She preferred to handle the matter herself."

"Vigilante justice, eh?" He tsked. "We can't have that, now can we?"

"I'd hardly call it vigilante justice, Your Honor. She was merely defending herself against an unwanted advance."

"I beg to differ. She wasn't defending herself at all. She was giving retribution." His gaze zeroed in on Viv. "And that's not for her to decide. That's up to the court. Or, more specifically, *me*."

"But your honor—"

"Enough Ms. Waverly," he said, perusing the paperwork in front of him. "I've made my decision. Given the evidence here, I have no choice but to find Ms. Foster guilty of the charge against her. We can't have women walking about the city clobbering every man who makes a harmless pass at her. It's unseemly."

Harmless pass? Viv thought. The cretin *had grabbed her ass*. It wasn't as if he'd merely smiled at her. This was total bullshit. She opened her mouth to tell him so, but stopped when Minna's fingernails dug into her arm. "Don't," her friend whispered, giving her head an almost imperceptible shake.

"Justice should be left to those who have the power to dispense it." He looked up at Viv and grinned. "I'm sentencing you to forty hours of community service at Bailey's Tree Farm. That should put you more in a proper Christmas spirit."

A tree farm? she thought, reeling. He couldn't be serious. She didn't know how to chop down a tree, much less possess the strength to drag one out of the forest and haul it onto someone's freaking car. She had little hands and she hated being cold. This couldn't be right. It had to be a mistake.

Bailey's Farm wasn't completely unknown to her though— her mother faithfully bought her tree there every year and had always made a grand outing of it with her children when they'd been at home. Unbidden, Viv had a startlingly clear image of a tall skinny boy with dark brown hair and pale gray eyes.

"Hopefully a little bit of Christmas spirit will rub off on you, and you'll think twice before assaulting another friendly young man." He rubbed his jaw as though it still hurt. "See my clerk and she'll get you squared away." He banged his gavel with particular relish. "Next case."

Minna quickly gathered her things and nudged Viv from behind the desk. "Let's go."

"But—" Guilty. Sentenced to work on a tree farm. By the very jerk who'd grabbed her ass in the first place, she was certain of it.

"I'm sorry," Minna said, herding her to the back of the courtroom and out the door as Viv dug in her heels and glared at the so-called judge. She *knew* it was him. How? That part was a little elusive, but she didn't doubt it all the same.

With another one of those smug smiles, he waved his fingers at her.

"We can appeal, right? You can get me out of this, can't you?"

Minna shook her head. "I don't think so." She grimaced and gave her head a puzzled shake. "He'd made up his mind before we ever came into the court room."

"That's because he's Damon Claus. Or his twin brother. Or something."

"Be that as it may, you're stuck, Viv. At this point I think you're better off just doing the community service and letting this go."

"Have you ever heard of anybody getting sentenced to doing community service at a tree farm?" she asked incredulously. Was the guy on crack? What sort of punishment was that?

Minna accepted Viv's paperwork from the clerk, then started down the long hall which led out to the parking lot. "You can't possibly tell me you'd rather put on an orange vest and pick up trash from along the side of the road than work at a tree farm?" she said.

"Well, no," Viv admitted. "Not when you put it that way." Still…she couldn't shake the feeling that she'd been seriously played.

Minna's steps slowed and an even slower grin Viv didn't altogether trust spread over her friend's lips. "In fact, there are definitely worse ways to pay your debt to society than getting to work side by side with Hank Bailey."

She frowned. "Sorry?"

"Hank Bailey. He helps me find my Christmas tree every year. Honestly, watching that man in action is one of the highlights of my Christmas season. He's the main reason that I haven't caved to convenience and bought an artificial tree. Are you telling me you've never been out to Bailey's Tree Farm?"

"You know I don't put up a tree," Viv said. Her only decorations were a paper wreath her nieces had made her out of their handprints, and a pretty snow globe of London's Hyde Park in winter that her mother had given her a few years ago for Christmas, along with the note, "Someday…"

That someday, provided nothing went wrong, was December 26. She'd been steadily saving for a couple of years now, determined to make the trip. But every time she got close to her goal amount, something invariably went wrong. To date that London fund had absorbed the cost of a new hot water heater and repairs to her transmission in her car.

But not this year. This year she was going.

She didn't know why it had suddenly become so important that she do it now, but she couldn't shake it. The idea of bringing in another New Year—on the heels of the Most Miserable Time of The Year—as someone's lonely, pathetic guest made her absolutely heartsick.

She *needed* to go away. She *needed* London.

"I know you don't put up a tree now, Ms. Scrooge, but what about when you were a kid? I know I've run into your mother at Bailey's before."

"Mom gets her tree there every year," Viv said, once again besieged by the image of that gangly teenage boy with the pale gray eyes. Hank Bailey? she wondered, slightly in-trigued.

Minna looked at her watch. "Sorry, sweetie. I've got to meet a client." She handed Viv the papers. "You start on Monday, 8:00 a.m. I'll give you a call later."

Viv thanked her friend and watched her leave. It wasn't until the doors closed behind Minna's retreating back that her words fully surfaced. She felt her eyes widen in horror, then looked down at the orders in her hand.

*Monday through Friday, 8:00 a.m.–4:00 p.m.*

She was supposed to be at work from 8:00 a.m.–4:00 p.m. How in the hell was she supposed to be two places at once?

A fatalistic laugh bubbled up her throat.

She couldn't.

Goodbye, London. *Again.*

# 2

"I JUST DON'T believe you," Jason said, shaking his head. "Amanda's pretty. She's smart. She's funny. Have I mentioned she's pretty? And *you* don't like her." He blew out a sigh of exasperated air. "Why the hell not, Hank? What's wrong with this one?"

Henry "Hank" Livingston Bailey—named after the true author of *The Night Before Christmas*—ignored the familiar tirade altogether. "Instead of worrying about my love life, why don't you help me get this tree onto the stand?"

Grumbling under his breath, Jason, his younger, recently-happily-married brother did as he was told. "You don't have a love life to worry about," he said, positioning the blue spruce. "You have a series of let's-see dinners that always result in the woman of the hour not passing muster." Jase shook his head. "I just don't get it. What was wrong with this one, bro? Was her nose a little off-center like the last chick? Was she a 'loud-chewer' like the one before that?" Jason snorted. "Honestly, you go into a date looking for a reason to bail. I don't know why you even bother."

Frankly, he was beginning to wonder the same thing, Hank thought, spinning the tree to inspect it for imperfections. He trimmed the top and tidied a section near the bottom, before gesturing to the guys to take it to the lot.

While most customers liked to stroll around the farm in search of their own tree, there were several people who preferred to browse their pre-cut selection, then retire into the gift shop for hot apple cider or chocolate—whatever they preferred—and a homemade iced sugar cookie.

In addition to those items, his mother and sister baked holiday offerings—his mother's pecan pie being a favorite— and stocked the store with handmade Christmas ornaments. To say that Bailey's Tree Farm was anything short of a family affair would be a huge understatement. Even Jason's new bride, Angelica, had been pressed into service creating a new brochure for the business and, more recently, had been helping out in the gift shop.

Despite the fact that Christmas only came once a year, the farm was a year-long job. In addition to servicing the greater Jackson area, Bailey's shipped trees all over the southeast. When the official season was over, the real work began. Stumps had to be removed, new trees planted, weed control, insect and disease maintenance, shaping. Since it took five to seven years to produce the typical six- to seven-foot tree, their business plan was always working seven years in advance. There was never what one would call a "down time." It was hard work, but it was lucrative thanks to the increasing commercialism of the season. He had to admit he hated that part, but it left him feeling a bit like a hypocrite if he complained.

But how in the hell, in the middle of all that effort and planning, was he supposed to find time to date, much less find someone he wanted to spend the rest of his life with?

"So tell me, what was wrong with Amanda?" Jase persisted. "I want to make sure we don't try to hook you up with anyone who has the same problem."

Hank wrangled another tree onto the stand and started the process all over again. "Here's a thought. Why don't you stop trying to hook me up with anyone?"

Jase grinned. "No can do, bro. Angelica is convinced that

you're going to make some lucky woman very happy. She thinks it's a crime that you're old and alone."

Hank chuckled. He would cop to being alone, but old? He was thirty. Hardly ancient, by anyone's standards. His gaze slid to Jase and his lips quirked. Unless it was his twenty-one-year old little brother and his equally young new wife. No doubt to them, he was just one fiber bar short of the old folks' home.

Still, he knew his brother well enough to know that unless he answered him, this line of questioning would continue ad nauseum, so he was better off to simply lay it all out on the line.

"You want to know what was wrong with her?"

Jase's eyes widened comically. "Isn't that what I've been asking you for the past fifteen minutes?"

"Thirty," he corrected. "It's been thirty minutes. After five minutes of your incessant nosiness my eye starts to twitch. After ten I want to go deaf. At fifteen I'm considering permanently removing your vocal cords and after thirty I'm on the brink of throttling you senseless. Since the impulse to wrap my hands around your scrawny little neck is at maximum capacity, I know it's been *thirty* minutes."

Jase merely smiled. "What happens after an hour?"

"Your wife becomes a widow and I become a permanent stain on the family name."

"That would be tragic."

Hank laughed softly. "Smart-ass."

"Well?" his brother prodded.

Hank leaned against the log planks of their shaping shed and picked the pine needles out of his gloves. "She told me that she doesn't like a 'real' Christmas tree. That the scent of evergreen reminds her of those bad air fresheners in public restrooms."

Jase, recognizing an unforgivable Bailey sin, whistled low. *"Damn."*

Hank smirked. "She's got a pre-lit artificial Douglas fir,

Jase." He pushed away from the wall, preparing to go back to work before they officially opened for business. "Any woman who doesn't like the scent of evergreen and uses a *fake tree* for Christmas isn't the woman for me."

And that was putting it mildly. In all seriousness, whoever the future Mrs. Bailey turned out to be, she needed to love Christmas as much as he did. Christmas wasn't just a season—it was his livelihood. His heritage. He glanced around, taking in the acres and acres of trees in various stages of growth.

Bailey's had been farming this land for more than one-hundred years. His great-grandfather had bought the property with the intent to farm cotton, but the ground had been a bit too rocky. His wife had noticed the native Scotch pines grew quite prettily and had suggested letting families come out and cut their trees at Christmas as a way to bring in some extra cash. Her suggestion had turned into a profitable business that had been handed down for the past three generations. To this day, they still used his great-grandmother's sugar cookie recipe to offer to their customers.

"I'm sorry, Hank. That sucks. I was hoping she might be the one."

Hank shrugged. He was beginning to wonder if The One existed. For all of his complaining about his brother butting into his romance life, Hank had to admit that he'd begun to seriously miss being in a committed relationship.

He had been, once.

He'd been in his early twenties, just out of college and had fallen ass over end for a girl who worked for their local radio station selling advertising. Hell, even her name had been perfect. Noelle.

Unfortunately, while Hank had been thinking happily-ever-after, Noelle had been secretly balling her much older—and richer—boss. Who was married. The boss left his wife and family for Hank's faithless girlfriend and, as far as Hank knew, they were still together.

Needless to say, the whole experience had left him with a bad taste in his mouth and a general distrust for women that he hadn't been completely successful in shaking. Like Jason said, he managed to always find fault and he knew that the fear of getting hurt was no small part of the problem.

Furthermore, though it shouldn't matter how he met his Ms. Right, Hank longed for a more "organic" meeting. Despite all logic, he clung to the idealistic idea that he would simply *know* when he found the right girl for him. Irrational? Pathetically romantic? Unrealistic?

Yes, to all of the above.

But he couldn't shake the notion, no matter how impractical it might seem.

"Hank?"

Hank's gaze swung to Brody Foster, one of the troubled teens who'd been working on the farm since the beginning of summer. Hank had a soft spot, in particular, for this kid, who had an absentee father and a harried, mostly-disinterested mother who couldn't be bothered to care for him. Like most teenagers who were left to their own devices, Brody had developed a talent for getting into trouble. No drugs, thank God. Just your typical run-of-the-mill, thug-in-the-making behavior. Since he'd been working here though, the boy seemed more focused and appeared to be doing better.

"Yeah?" Hank said.

"Your mother told me to tell you that the lady who's supposed to do her community service work is here."

Jason perked up. "The Santa Slugger? She's here now?"

Brody grinned. "Yes, sir."

Vivian Foster—aka The Santa Slugger—had become a hot topic of conversation ever since last week when Hank had gotten a call from Judge Moroz's clerk about possibly accommodating him in a community service project. Though he'd thought it a bit of an odd request, Hank imagined that his work with the local teen center had prompted the idea.

Furthermore, what better place for a woman who'd attacked Santa Claus to do her community service than at a Christmas tree farm? Hank grinned. This Judge Moroz had a very interesting sense of humor.

"What's she like?" Jason wanted to know.

"Short," Brody told him. "It's hard to imagine her laying into Big Red."

"Don't let her size fool you," Jase said, chuckling darkly. "It's the small ones you have to look out for. They've usually got a terrible temper."

Hank felt a smile tug at his lips. "Are you referring to our mother or your wife?"

"Both."

Hank was inclined to agree. His mother was as loving as the day was long, but when she got angry… She was like a little tornado, wreaking havoc on everything around her. He hadn't seen Angelica display that sort of a temper yet, but no doubt his brother had and from the look on Jason's face, he actually liked the occasional storm. Moonstruck moron, Hank thought, peeling off his gloves.

"She's in the gift shop, then?"

"Yes, sir."

"Thanks for letting me know, Brody. I'll head over there now." He started toward the small gingerbread-type cottage that housed their bakery and gift shop.

"I'll come with you," Jason piped up, falling into step beside him. "I want to get a look at this girl."

"She's not here for your entertainment. She's here to work."

"Yes, for free. I like her already, don't you?"

Hank stifled a smile. "It's not for free. She's fulfilling her debt to society."

"Well, I'm glad that she's paying it here. Lately Angelica's been a little too tired to—" He cleared his throat and the tops of his ears turned pink. "An extra pair of hands in the gift shop will be nice. I know they can use the help."

"Who says she's going to get a cushy job in the gift shop?" Hank asked. "Judge Moroz indicated that he wanted this to be unpleasant for her so that she doesn't become a repeat offender."

"A repeat offender?" he asked, his eyes widening. "You think she's going to become some sort of serial Santa slugger? She's going to travel from mall to mall attacking hired Saint Nick's?" He snorted.

Hank would admit it was a bit of a stretch. Still, he'd given his word that he would make her work in every area of the farm, not just the gift shop. Naturally, how long she worked in each position was at his discretion, but he certainly wasn't going to ignore his promise.

"What if she's old? You're going to make some short old lady help cut down trees?"

"Of course not." But, for whatever reason, he hadn't gotten the impression that she was an "old lady." He mounted the steps to the gift shop, then pulled open the door and stepped inside.

A blanket of warmth washed over him and the familiar scent of cinnamon, sugar and cider reached his senses. No matter how many times he'd come into this shop, he never failed to appreciate the very essence of Christmas it evoked. A cozy blaze crackled in the stacked stone fireplace, holiday music played from hidden speakers and the occasional blow of the horn from the antique train set that circled on a specially built track near the ceiling always made him feel like a kid again. How could anyone not like Christmas? Hank wondered. It was the most wonderful time of the year. He breathed deeply…then completely lost his breath as the Santa Slugger turned around.

His body went into an instant, scorching full-on burn. A tingly wave of prickly sensation started at the bottoms of his feet and swept upward, followed by an all over shiver he could thankfully blame on the cold.

One look, a mere three seconds in her company and he wanted her more than he'd ever wanted anything in his life. She was sexual perfection. Utterly gorgeous. He went instantly hard, just looking at her.

"Ah, here he is now," he heard his mother say, seemingly from very far away.

Her eyes were the most curious shade of blue he'd ever seen. Deep, almost purple, sparkling with intelligence. Heavily fringed with long lashes, they put him in mind of sugared violets, which somehow seemed appropriate because every inch of her was utterly delectable. She was short, but extremely curvy—particularly her rump. Jet black curly hair tumbled almost to her shoulders beneath a charming red beret. She had smooth ivory skin, rosy plump cheeks, a tiny little nose and a pair of mouth-wateringly perfect Cupid's bow lips. She put him in mind of one of his mother's china dolls, only fully grown and sexy as hell.

For starters, his mother's dolls didn't have breasts.

A flash of what looked like recognition lit her unusual gaze, but Hank was certain he'd never met her before.

He wouldn't have forgotten.

He extended his hand and the moment her dainty little fingers closed over his, a jolt of indefinable emotion traveled up his arm along with the electrical current that rooted his feet to the floor and made every hair on his head prickle with awareness.

And in that instant *he knew.* Call it intuition, call it psychic ability, call it shades of Tom Hanks in *Sleepless In Seattle.* *He knew.*

There would be no finding fault with this woman because every cell in his body told him she was absolutely perfect.

He wanted her. And he *would* have her.

# 3

IT WAS HIM, Viv thought as that vaguely familiar smile shaped the sexiest masculine mouth she'd ever had the pleasure to gaze upon. Slightly crooked, inherently open and at once endearing.

Her shallow breath stuttered out of her lungs and a bolt of heat landed in her womb. Impossibly, her breasts ripened in her bra and an unmistakably current of need coiled low in her belly. It was him, only the mature version. Six and a half feet of rugged, muscled, flannel and denim-clad male. The scent of cedar clung to him along with something else, an intriguing combination of citrus and patchouli. It made her want to lean into him and then lick the side of his neck. Her lips quirked.

Of course, she should probably shake his hand first.

His big hand closed over hers and she had the oddest sensation of both simultaneously falling and taking root. Her feet felt like they'd been cemented to the floor, while the rest of her body seemed to be floating. The air around them seemed to thicken with awareness and she was struck with the curious urge to reach up and thread her fingers through his wavy dark brown locks. The contrast between the rich shade of his hair and those pale gray eyes was unbelievably striking, leaving her a bit breathless.

"Hank Bailey," he said, his smooth baritone sliding over her like warm caramel. "You must be Vivian."

"Viv, please," she automatically corrected. "The only

person who ever calls me Vivian is my mother and it's usually when I've done something to incur her wrath."

His smile widened and he jerked his head toward his own mother, a spry sixty something with graying hair and keen blue eyes. "She's been known to call me Henry on occasion, so I know exactly what you mean."

"I only call him Henry when he deserves it," his mother interjected. "Thankfully it isn't that often."

"Whereas I get the full name treatment on a daily basis," a younger, shorter version of Hank said, striding forward to shake her hand, as well. "I'm Jason Bailey." He gestured to a pretty blonde behind the counter. "That's my wife, Angelica."

"Circumstances aside, it's a pleasure to meet you," Viv said, charmed in spite of herself. She'd had to kiss her London vacation goodbye to serve her community service—her manager at the mall wouldn't give her the week off and instead had immediately hired her replacement—so she'd been in a sour mood over the weekend, one which had reached maximum capacity by the time she'd gotten into her car to make the drive out here this morning. She'd been determined to hate every moment of this, but it was clear that spending a week with this family—her gaze slid to Hank—might be more…tolerable than she anticipated.

Hank blinked as though he'd just remembered something, then stepped back and drew a young man forward. She pegged him as an early teen. He was in that gangly stage, where his skin hadn't quite caught up with his body. He was tall and rather thin, but the promise of manhood lurked in the breadth of his shoulders and the strong line of his spottily shaved jaw.

"And this is Brody," Hank said, slapping the kid on the back. "He's my right-hand man around here."

The boy blushed at the praise, giving the impression that he wasn't used to receiving compliments. Her heart instantly ached for the kid and she instinctively wanted to comfort him. Furthermore, there was something vaguely familiar about him. She couldn't put her finger on it, but she had the peculiar sensation that she'd seen him before. That she should know him. She'd probably run into him at the mall, Viv decided. After all, it was one of the local hangouts for Jackson's youth.

She smiled. "Sounds like you've got an important job about here."

He nodded. "I try."

"Brody's a hard worker," Hank said.

Viv took an expectant breath and rocked back slightly on her heels. "Speaking of work, I should probably get started, right?"

Hank rubbed the back of his neck, as though he was reluctant to assign her a task. No doubt when he'd volunteered to use his business for community service workers, he'd expected to get strapping young guys who'd be able to chop down trees and do a bit of heavy lifting. Well, she might be small, but she was tough. Not that she particularly *wanted* to work outside and cut down a tree. But if she had to, she could, if nothing else than to prove to this guy she wasn't a total lightweight.

"How about I take you around the farm and show you how everything works first?"

She nodded. "Sure."

His mother hurried around the counter and pressed a cup of hot apple cider into her hands. "You're going to need this, dear. It's cold out there this morning."

Viv murmured a thanks, then followed Hank outside. The air had a bite to it that made her want to instantly retreat back into the cozy, sweet-smelling gift shop. But the idea of walking around with Hank warmed her from the inside so she fell into step beside him.

"I used to come here when I was a kid," Viv said.

"Oh, really?"

"Yeah. My mother still visits every year and gets her tree. Leila Foster?"

Recognition flashed in those unique gray eyes and he smiled. "Seven-and-half-foot Douglas fir every time." He nodded. "Picky, your mom, but she has a great eye."

"She loves to decorate for Christmas and thinks it's sacrilegious to use an artificial tree."

He opened the door to his truck for her and she caught another tantalizing whiff of his scent. Her mouth actually watered. "Then we're of the same mind, then," he said. He jerked his head, indicating the farm. "My living depends on people like your mom."

Considering it was such a seasonal business, she could completely understand that. For the first time in her adult life, she felt sort of bad for never buying a Christmas tree. Of course, one would have to actually like Christmas to want a tree, and considering that the holiday had been forever tainted by her cheating bastard of a father, she'd never seen the need. Typically she just gritted her teeth and got through the season.

Thanksgiving was actually her holiday of choice and she had the decorations to prove it. Cornucopias, pumpkins, fall garlands and mums. It was an unsung, largely neglected and glossed over occasion, a speed bump, if you will, along the commercialized road to the Christmas season. She liked the message behind the Thanksgiving holiday, to be appreciative of what one has without having to donate a gift in the process.

Hank slipped into the driver's seat, quickly cranked the truck, then adjusted the heat. "Sorry," he said. "It'll take it a minute to warm up. I've been down here since five this morning."

She felt her eyes round. "Five?" And as for the heat, she was warm enough already. He was making her quite…hot.

"We start early during the busy season. In addition to the

local farm, we ship trees to a lot of the home improvement stores in the south east. We farm roughly three thousand acres and the majority of that land is used for our commercial business."

"Wow," she said, impressed. "I had no idea."

He pointed to a medium-size log cabin with a long porch. Jason and Brody were busy trimming a tree and offered a wave as they drove past. She experienced a bit of déjà vu, looking at Brody again. She definitely knew him. But from where?

"That's the trimming shed. Once they've gotten the tree into an acceptable shape, they'll run it through the netting machine to make it easier for customers to transport home. We sell our own stands, as well. They're heavier, better weighted than any of those flimsy things you'll get in a store."

She felt a smile flirt with her lips. "Are you trying to sell me one?"

He negotiated a turn and trees of varying sizes laid out in neat rows all around them. In the distance a large barn, presumably with maintenance equipment, loomed in the distance along with various other little buildings.

He shot her a grin. "Only if you need one. But I'm partial to ours because I designed it."

Impressed, she nodded. "I'll definitely have to check it out, then."

He drove down several little gravel roads, pointing out various structures on the property and explaining their purpose, then took her through each section of farm, showcasing the variety of trees they grew and sold on the property.

"Blue spruce, Scotch pine, Douglas fir, a few cedar," he said. "Despite the fact that it's not as pretty a green as the Scotch pine, I'm a blue spruce fan. They're easy to shape and have good, sturdy limbs."

Clearly he was passionate about what he did, Viv noted,

charmed. He knew his business and seemed genuinely taken with his profession. In her experience, that was an increasingly rare thing. Most men of her acquaintance were simply working to get paid and took little notice, much less pride, in how they made their living.

They crested a hill and several houses came into view. He drew to a stop, then nodded toward an old two-story antebellum house. "That was my great-grandfather's place. He was the one who started it all. My parents live there now. Both my brother and I have built out here, as well."

She could see that. There were two other houses, both of them large and roomy, not exactly what one would have pictured for either a newly married couple or a bachelor like Hank—she'd covertly checked his ring finger after he'd finished shaking her hand. Clearly these homes had been built with future families in mind. For reasons she couldn't explain, a small lump formed in her throat. These men didn't think in the short term, Viv realized, another increasingly rare trait.

"The dark green cedar with the white trim is mine," Hank told her. "And see those little orange flags out there in the middle of that field?"

Viv nodded. "That's our future community playhouse. We're putting in a big recreation room with a kitchen to accommodate holidays and get-togethers and the like, as well as a pool."

She chuckled softly and inclined her head. "Building your own family subdivision, eh?"

He returned her grin. "We like to think of it as a compound," he said. "You know, sort of like the Kennedys', just on a smaller scale."

"It's lovely," she told him, meaning it.

The radio Hank had stashed in the cup holder suddenly sounded. "Hank, are you going to dawdle around all day flirting with our new worker or are you going to get back here and log in some true time?" Jason asked.

Unbelievably, Hank blushed, and that little bit of pink in his cheeks delighted her beyond reason. "Excuse me," he said, shooting her a sheepish smile. "We're on our way back now," he told him. "Keep your skirt on." He glanced at her. "Sorry about that. My brother fancies himself a comedian."

"No problem. I've got a sister who has a similar tendency."

His eyes twinkled. "I've got to tell you, you've been quite a little celebrity around here for the past week."

"Really?"

"Yeah. It's not every day we get a woman who's doing community service out here for h-hitting Santa C-Claus," he said, chuckling under his breath. "Jase has been calling you the Santa Slugger."

Viv rolled her eyes, slightly mortified. "Excellent. A nickname. I'll have you know that until this incident, my record was clean. This is my first ever stint in community service."

"Well, you're not sporting any gang tattoos and don't seem to be pierced in any of the unusual places. You look pretty even-tempered," he said, his gaze skimming over her. That casual perusal made her skin prickle and her neck go warm. "So…what happened? Why did you feel the need to deck old Saint Nick?"

She frowned. "You mean you don't know?"

"No. That wasn't included in any of the paperwork the court sent over."

She rolled her eyes. "Of course not. Leave it to that joke of a judge to leave out anything that would have painted me in a better light."

"Are you saying you weren't guilty?"

"No," she admitted, expelling a disgusted breath. "I *did* hit him. And I'd do it again in the heartbeat under the same circumstances."

A puzzled line emerged between his brows.

Oh, for pity's sake. "You really want to know why I did it?"

He poked his tongue in his cheek. "I'll admit I'm intrigued."

Viv released another prolonged breath. "Fine. I'll tell you why. I did it because Santa Claus grabbed my ass."

# 4

HANK BLINKED. "Come again?"

"He grabbed my ass," she repeated, a trace of outrage in her voice. "The guy was a mall Santa and he'd been following me around for a couple of weeks, leering at me and making suggestive comments. But when he decided to cop a feel, I rounded on him." She smiled unrepentantly. "Like I said, I'd do it again."

"And the judge found you guilty?"

Her lips slid into a hard smile. "I'm relatively certain that the judge who sentenced me was the same guy I cold-cocked."

Shocked, Hank shook his head. "You're kidding me."

"I wish."

Hank didn't know what he'd expected her to say, but getting felt up by Santa Claus certainly wasn't in any scenario he'd imagined. Stunned, he simply shook his head. "But what about your attorney? Couldn't he do anything?"

"*She* did the best she could." Viv let go a sigh and gestured wearily. "And the truth is I *did* hit him. I was guilty of assault."

Hank drummed his fingers against the steering wheel. "Yeah, but there were extenuating circumstances. You shouldn't have to do this." And he certainly didn't like the part he was playing in her punishment. On the other hand, she was the most exciting thing that had happened to him in recent memory, so selfishly he was glad to have her here. He'd never had such a visceral reaction to a woman before and, while he was certainly no genius, he had sense enough to know that this was important.

"I agree," she said. "But this is just the way it is. Honestly, I just want to do my time, so to speak, and move on."

A thought struck. "So you work at the mall, then?"

Another smile that didn't quite ring true shaped her distractingly pretty mouth. "I did."

Damn, he didn't like the sound of that. A bad feeling formed in his gut. "Did?" Past tense. Not good.

"They wouldn't let me off for a week, so they've hired a replacement."

Though this was in no way his fault, Hank couldn't help feeling guilty all the same. His shoulders rounded as he let out a breath. "I'm sorry, Viv," he said, for lack of anything better.

She waved off his concern with one of her tiny hands. He loved those dainty little fingers and was suddenly struck with a vision of them sliding over his naked skin, kneading his shoulders and drifting over his chest. He sucked a slow breath through his teeth and tried to focus.

"Don't worry about it," she told him. "It was just a parttime gig to cover Christmas and take myself on a little vacation. I'm actually in Web site design, so it's not like I lost my only means of income."

Maybe so, Hank thought, but from the hauntingly sad look around her eyes, she'd lost something equally, if not more, important. He was hit with the sudden urge to fix things for her. How? Why? Who the hell knew? He just wanted to be her hero.

And as it happened, the family had been planning to build a Web site for their business. It was past time, really, and if he hired her to do the work, then she'd be able to recoup the lost wages. He pulled back up in front of the gift shop and shifted into Park, but didn't readily kill the engine.

"It's slow right now. Always is around Christmas," she explained. A smile tugged at her lips. "People are buying Christmas trees and presents and traveling to see their families. They're not interested in building a new site or getting a redesign."

"I am," Hank told her, making an executive decision. His father, who was currently away at the moment courting new business, had long ago put Hank in charge.

Those purple eyes widened. "What?"

He gestured toward the farm. "We've been talking about putting a site up for over a year now, but haven't taken the time to get it done. Would you be interested?"

The look she gave him made his chest swell with masculine pleasure. "Certainly. Do you have time to tell me what you'd want?"

Hank winced. "Not at the moment, but maybe we could discuss it over dinner?"

She smiled hesitantly. "I don't have any plans."

Inwardly he gave a little cheer. "Good. Why don't you come up to my house this evening when we finish for the day and I'll throw something together for us."

"You're going to cook?"

Hank chewed the inside of his cheek. "It's how I usually feed myself."

She laughed. "I'm sorry. I know I shouldn't be shocked, but…"

"But I'm a guy and I'm supposed to be helpless in the kitchen and incapable of picking out coordinating fabrics?"

She laughed again, a delighted chuckle that made his stomach flutter and his dick stir beneath his boxers. He wanted to hear that laugh in bed, while they were both naked.

"The fact that you know that fabrics *can* coordinate sets you apart from the average male already."

His gaze tangled purposely with hers. "Good. I don't like being average."

A small breath stuttered out of her lungs and the climate instantly changed in the cab of his truck. "An over-achiever, are you?"

"I pride myself on doing things well."

She swallowed, seemed to lean toward him a bit, though that could only be wishful thinking on his part. "It's a g-good trait."

He shrugged as though it was difficult to be this perfect, purposely trying to make her laugh again. "I've been told I've got a few."

Her lips twitched. "Mother's often praise their children."

A burst of laughter rumbled up his throat. "Too true," he conceded, enjoying himself more than he had in years.

A knock sounded at his window, startling him. Hank swore, then turned to see his brother standing there. "You want to get out the truck, your majesty, and help around here, or do you want us peasants to do all the work?"

Hank sighed. "Do you see what I have to deal with?"

She nodded once, her lips twitching. "I do."

"I suppose I should get back to work." He didn't want to, though. He'd rather enjoy her company, fall into those deep purple eyes and coax a kiss from that unapologetically sexy mouth. He knew instinctively that she'd be a good kisser, that she would welcome his hands on her face, that she would fit perfectly against him. Another bolt of heat landed in his loins, making him shift in his seat. This was ridiculous. He was ready to detonate right now, yet he hadn't officially even initiated the launch sequence.

"What do you want me to do?"

*Aside crawl into my lap?* Hank thought. "Work with my mother in the gift shop. We'll count the tour as your day in the field."

She frowned. "What?"

"Judge Moroz specifically asked that you work in the field and on the lot."

Her eyes sparked with irritation. "Really? Is that normal?"

"What do you mean?"

"I mean do judges usually make those kinds of requests?"

Hank shrugged. "I wouldn't know. You're the first person who's ever served their community service here."

"The first?"

"Yeah. I work with several guidance counselors at the local junior high and high schools, bringing unruly kids out here to work in lieu of detention, giving them something to do besides get into more trouble. But you're the first community service worker we've had." He smiled. "Frankly, it was a little strange. Judge Moroz's clerk called last week and set this up."

"Oh." She chewed her bottom lip thoughtfully. "Do you remember what day she called?"

"Wednesday," Hank said.

She inclined her head and an ironic laugh slipped between her lips. It made him distinctly uneasy. "Well, that explains it, then."

Hank quirked a brow. "Explains what?"

"Why my lawyer thought the judge had made up his mind before he even heard my case. I was in court on Thursday and he'd already arranged my sentence before I got there." She laughed again and shook her head. "Looks like I picked the wrong mall Santa to deck, didn't I?"

"You should report him," Hank said, angered on her behalf. "This isn't right."

Viv shook her head, sending an errant curl against her bottom lip where it clung distractingly. "No," she said, sighing. "Ordinarily I would agree and quite frankly, the idea of finding him and pummeling him again for good measure is incredibly tempting, but...I think I need to put my head down and stay off his radar." She looked up and grinned. "It's only a week and you've given me a new job. It's all good."

He nodded, irrationally pleased. "Good."

"So, just leave here at four and go to your house?"

Hank nodded. "That'll work."

"I'll see you then." Viv slid out of truck and made her way toward the gift shop.

Hank exited, as well, and, whistling tunelessly, sidled over to the trim shed to help his irritating little brother.

"What the hell took you so long?" Jase demanded. "We're freezing our ass hairs off out here while you're riding around in your heated truck with a hot girl, you giant dipstick."

Hank ignored him.

"Well? What were you doing?"

"Making dinner plans," Hank told him.

Jase's mouth sagged open. "Dinner plans? Are you telling me you've asked her out already?"

Hank looked over toward the gift shop and from his vantage point he watched his mother put an apron over Viv's head. The tableau made something near his heart shift. She fit here. She belonged. It was completely irrational, but he knew it all the same. "I did," he confirmed, resisting the urge to smile like a total nimrod. "Boys," he confided with a slap on Jason and Brody's back. "I think I've got a crush on the Santa Slugger."

# 5

THOUGH SHE'D BEEN TEMPTED to join Maureen, Hank's mother, and Angelica for lunch, Viv had taken the opportunity to run home and snag her laptop for her dinner meeting with Hank this evening.

Dinner. Alone. With him.

This felt distinctly like a date.

She resisted the urge to squeal with delight—ordinarily she was not a squealer, delighted or otherwise—but something about Hank Bailey made her want to turn up her *Sound of Music* CD and whirl around her living room, singing the lyrics at the top of her lungs.

That track would be immediately followed by Marvin Gaye's "Let's Get It On."

Honestly, she had never in her life looked at a guy and instantly thought about taking all of his clothes off, then licking him from one end to the other. She'd never gotten wet from a mere handshake and she sure as hell had never considered making sure she was wearing her "good" underwear on a first date.

Until now.

Hank Bailey was a hundred percent *male*. In a time when men were waxing their eyebrows, getting manicures and pedicures, spa treatments and their hair highlighted, Hank was a refreshing throwback to when men were just men.

And he was one helluva specimen. His shoulders... She'd

spent the day covertly watching him work and had had the pleasure of witnessing those broad, muscled shoulders in action. On more than one occasion, she'd imagined gently biting one.

Clearly she'd lost her mind.

Viv let out a shaky breath, wiped a bead of sweat from her upper lip as she let herself into her small Craftman's style home a few blocks away from one of Jackson's historic district. Though it had required eating more noodles than she ever would have thought possible, and cutting her phone and cable services to the bone for years on end—with the exception of graduating from college with no student loans—nothing had ever made Viv prouder than purchasing her first home.

She loved her little house and had painstakingly worked to restore it to its former beauty. With lots of hardwood, crown molding and built-ins, the old house had more character than any of the new boxy-type cookie cutter homes going up in some of the trendier subdivisions.

Her cat, Geraldine, named after her favorite character from the British comedy *The Vicar of Dibley,* curled around her legs and howled her displeasure. No doubt her bowl was empty again. Much like her namesake, Geraldine had a fondness for food. Viv set her purse aside and dropped a few pieces of kibble into the cat's bowl. "That'll have to do until I get home this evening," she said, then bent and scratched the fat tabby behind the ears. Momentarily satisfied, the spoiled feline purred in appreciation.

A quick glance at the clock confirmed that she needed to get back on the road, so rather than linger over her cat, she stood and quickly gathered her laptop and accessories. It would be nice if Hank had an internet connection, but she had much of her files stored onto this computer so that she could at least showcase a bit of her handiwork.

While she felt like he'd given her the business to offset

her lost income—an especially gallant thing to do—Viv wanted to make sure he knew that she knew what she was doing. If his business was as broad as he claimed—and he had no reason to lie—then a Web presence would be a serious boon to his company. In short, she'd make sure that he wasn't sorry.

Her gaze slid to her mantle, where her Hyde Park snow globe once more sparkled with promise. He wasn't just giving her the lost income—she'd gotten her vacation back.

*London. The day after Christmas.* She absolutely couldn't wait.

With only a few minutes to spare, Viv decided she'd take a chance and see if she could catch Minna to bring her up to speed on the recent developments. She caught her on her cell and relayed the information Hank had shared with her this morning regarding when Judge Moroz's clerk had contacted him.

Minna swore. "That unethical bastard. I'll have his job. I'll—"

"Don't," Viv told her. "It's fine."

"What do you mean it's fine? You're doing community service at a tree farm and you lost your job. You've kissed London goodbye again because you're too frugal to put a penny of the trip on a credit card. It's not fine. It's—"

Viv smiled. "Actually, London's back on and I daresay I'm going to bank more designing a site for Hank than I would have wrapping presents for another three weeks."

Minna grew quiet. "It's Hank now, is it? Do tell," she said in a sing-song voice. "I sense a story."

Viv laughed. "There's a bit of one. I'm having dinner with him tonight to go over content and design for his Web site. He's cooking for me."

"Excuse me," Minna said. "I need to see if I can find a concealer that will cover this unattractive shade of green I'm turning. Dinner, eh? And *he's* cooking?" She sighed wistfully.

"Gorgeous and capable. I knew there was more to that man than those impressive shoulders."

"His ass isn't half-bad, either," Viv said.

"Ogling already. No wonder you're content to serve your time."

She let go a small sigh and a secret thrill tingled in her palms. "Interestingly enough, I am."

"But you hate Christmas. How are you going to explain your aversion to Captain Christmas?"

"I'm not," Viv said. "In fact, I'm thinking of getting a tree this year."

Minna gasped. "Converted already? Seventeen years of I-hate-Christmas and all it's taken is a single morning at a tree farm with a good-looking tree farmer and a cup of hot apple cider?"

"I'm not converted," Viv protested. "I just think it'll look odd if I don't get a tree. He hates artificial trees and in all honestly, were I to ever decide to embrace the holiday, I'd like to think that I'd be a real-tree kind of person." Though her friend couldn't see her, she gave a little sanctimonious nod.

"Are you going to ask him to come decorate it with you?" Minna needled, managing to make the suggestion downright sexual.

"Minna."

"Don't 'Minna' me. You like this guy. You're charmed. I can tell."

There was no point in denying it. From the instant he'd walked into the room and enveloped her palm in his huge, calloused hand, she'd been inwardly simmering with longing. Her belly had gone all hot and heavy and the tips of her breasts had literally tingled when he'd touched her. He absolutely lit her up. Viv grimaced. And it had been so long since anyone had managed to do that, she'd thought her fuse had been permanently broken.

To be honest, Viv was always exceedingly cautious when it came to romance and that sort of timidity didn't translate into forming meaningful relationships. Not to lay everything at her father's door, but she suspected at least part of her trust issues stemmed from his abandonment. There was no denying that it had shaped her. When her father had walked out, he'd left her mother with two small children to care for, a mountain of debt and sixty-seven dollars in the checking account. She'd watched her mother work her fingers to the bone to take care of them, to dig her way out of that hole. There was no doubt in her mind that her inherent need to avoid debt stemmed from that stark lesson. Not permanently attaching herself to a man who could hurt her was another. But…

Sexual attraction and good looks aside, there was something else about Hank that drew her to him, made him all the more appealing. The curve of that endearing smile engendered trust and the strength in those shoulders let a woman know that he'd be capable in a crisis. Intelligence and humor sparkled in those keen gray eyes and his loyalty to his family, land and heritage was undeniably impressive.

He was the total package, Viv realized, and for the first time since this whole mall Santa fiasco started, she could actually see the silver lining in what she thought had been a terrible mistake. She grinned.

And, interestingly enough, that silver lining was the exact same shade as Hank Bailey's eyes.

# 6

"WHEN YOU TOLD ME you were going to cook for me, I have to admit I was a little skeptical," Viv said, reloading her spoon. "But this—" She grinned. "This is delicious."

Hank inclined his head. "I'm glad you approve. I'm a big fan of the crock pot, especially in the winter. I always come in from the farm starving to death and I want something hot and hearty right then. I make a lot of chili, roasts, stews and the like." He tipped his bottle of Guinness at her. "But I have to admit, this is one of my better dinners. So I'm glad that it's what I'd put on today before I asked you over."

She took a pull from her own beer. "And the homemade bread?"

He grinned. "I slipped up here and put it in the bread maker at lunch," he confessed.

"It's wonderful. I'd always thought about buying one of those machines, but wasn't sure they'd work." She dredged a crust through her Irish stew and popped the last bite into her mouth. "I'm sold."

So was he. On her.

No doubt about it, she was the most wonderful creature he'd ever had the pleasure of spending time with. She'd walked right into his house and immediately appreciated the things that he prided himself on. He'd taken a lot of time with the design, particularly in the kitchen. He'd installed a huge fireplace, had used antique copper tiles on the ceiling and had made sure that things were equally aesthetically pleasing and functional.

Viv had settled right in and looked so at home in his house he had the almost incredible thought that she was the final—ultimate—accessory to make everything complete. Crazy, he knew, especially since he'd just met her, but it didn't feel that way at all. Instead, he felt like he'd known her his entire life. Almost as though his soul recognized hers.

And God knows he wanted her with an intensity completely out of the realm of his experience. While Hank had always had as healthy a sex drive as any guy, he'd nevertheless been careful when selecting a lover. Frankly, release was easy enough without risking disease, and he'd always had a bit of an outdated mode of thinking when it came to sex. In other words, he didn't believe in casual sex. He had to like a woman before he lusted. Atypical of his gender, but…

With Viv, he'd liked and lusted simultaneously and instinctively, he knew that making love to her would be the single most incredible thing that had ever happened to him.

He didn't just want her—he *needed* her.

The only blip in the evening had come when she'd stood in front of his Christmas tree. A strange, almost sad, look had dimmed that sparkling dark blue gaze. Concerned, he'd asked her if something was wrong and she'd merely shaken her head and cited a haven't-finished-my-shopping excuse. For reasons he didn't understand, he'd gotten the distinct impression that she wasn't telling the complete truth.

"Well, I think I have everything I need to start roughing out your design," she said. "I'll work up a quote for you later tonight and bring it with me tomorrow if that works for you."

"Can you give me a ballpark estimate?"

She quoted a figure he found more than reasonable considering everything he'd asked for. She hesitated, bit her lip. "Typically I get half of that amount up front—just to make sure I'm not wasting my time—and half upon approval once everything goes live."

"No problem." He started to stand. "Do you need a check now?"

"No," she said, staying him with a single touch to his sleeve. "Tomorrow's fine. Do you mind if I bring my camera? Since this is a family business, I need to get pictures of all of you, as well as photos of the farm, gift shop and the trees, of course."

Hank grimaced. "You can take a picture of everything but me."

She chuckled. "Sorry, I have to have a picture of you. It's essential to the design."

Hank passed a hand over his face. "I *hate* having my picture taken."

"You sound like a woman."

He cut her a glance. "Impugning my masculinity? After I just fed you a wonderful meal?"

"Sorry," she said, her laughter warming him as surely as the fire in the grate.

"That's some thanks," he muttered, needling her. "Bake homemade bread. Think about making a cake. And for what? Sexist insults."

She laughed again. "You *thought* about making a cake?"

He nodded once. "I did."

"But?" she prodded.

"But I don't know how."

Her eyes widened. "You know how to make bread, cook stew and other complicated dinners, but you can't make a cake?"

He absently scratched his chest. "It's a tragedy, I know."

"Even I know how to make a cake," she said.

"Good. You can make one for me. Tomorrow night? Same time. I'll cook. You provide dessert."

Her mouth dropped open and she stared at him for a moment, then her eyes began to twinkle. "Why do I feel like I was just maneuvered by a master?"

He lifted his shoulder in an offhand shrug. "Not a master, just a guy who's highly motivated."

She cut him a sly smile, one that said she was enchanted, but didn't altogether trust him. "Yes, but motivated to do what?" she asked suspiciously.

Hank considered his answer. He could play off the moment with a glib flirtatious comment, or he could be honest. The truth had the potential to scare the hell out of her, but he suspected anything less wasn't going to be acceptable. He had to be forthright.

"Spend more time with you," he said, his gaze tangling with hers. "If you're agreeable, of course." *Shit.* "I probably should have asked this before, but…are you seeing someone?"

She gave a droll laugh. "No." She gaze met his. "You?"

"I wouldn't be making a play for you if that was the case."

She sighed, almost wistfully. "No, you wouldn't, would you?" She cocked her head. "Can I ask you something?"

"Sure."

"Why are you still single? You seem like a great guy."

A bark of laughter rumbled from his chest. "Was there supposed to be a compliment in there?"

Chuckling, she bit her bottom lip. "You know what I mean," she said. "You're smart, funny, handsome and accomplished. *And* you can bake bread. Some girl should have snatched you up already."

"The same could be said of you," he countered.

She grinned. "I hope I never have a girl try to snatch me up. I'd hate to have to hurt her feelings."

"You're enjoying this, aren't you?"

She nodded. "I am."

"I mean, why are you still single? Why hasn't some guy clubbed you over the head and dragged you into his cave?"

"Probably because I would club him back," she said, eyes twinkling. "As evidenced by my community service."

Hank laughed. "Too true." He toyed with the edge of his napkin and released a pent-up sigh. "To answer your original question, I've just never found the right girl. Whoever I settle down with has to want this life as much as I do, you know? This is a family business and I have to consider that when I'm dating someone."

A shadow moved behind her eyes. "So you're looking for a Mrs. Claus type?"

"If you mean do I want a plump, graying older woman who smells like sugar cookies, I've already got one of those in my life—my mother." He grinned and purposely let his gaze linger on her lips. She licked them and her pupils dilated. "I'm just looking for someone to share my life with. Someone who makes me feel alive. Someone who energizes me, who relaxes me, who will be my lover, my friend, my confidante and my partner. Someone who will help me fill this house with kids, who will rock with me on that big front porch when I'm old."

Viv released a small breath. "That's a t-tall order."

No doubt she could fill it, Hank thought. "That's why I'm still looking." He leaned forward and slid the pad of his thumb over her bottom lip. "But I believe that I've just narrowed the search." He gently slid his lips over hers, just the briefest kiss. "What do you say, Viv? Will you spend some time with me?" he whispered, a hairsbreadth from that sweet, tempting mouth.

She leaned closer, returned his gesture with the smallest brush of a kiss. "I don't have a Christmas tree," she said, as though that would make a difference.

Hank chuckled softly against her mouth, then framed her face with his hands. "No problem," he told her. "I can hook you up."

Then he slanted his lips over hers...and tasted forever.

# 7

*OH, SWEET LORD, could this man kiss,* Viv thought as she leaned forward and tangled her tongue around his. It was urgent and unhurried, desperate and divine and she'd never—*never*—enjoyed tasting a man as much as she did Hank Bailey. The heavy weight of wanting settled into her belly and slid purposely toward her sex. She could feel her pulse hammering in the heart of her womb, her nipples pearling against her bra. Her limbs were heavy but almost graceful as she twined them around his neck and drew him closer to her to deepen the kiss.

Hank's masculine purr of pleasure reverberated in her mouth, a growl of satisfaction that made her smile against his lips. He sucked her tongue into his mouth, feeding at her, then sampled her bottom lip, carefully probing the sensitive inside of her mouth.

Though she wasn't exactly certain how she got there, a moment later Viv was settled firmly in his lap. He tunneled his fingers into her hair, then kissed a path along her jawline and gently nipped at her ear. She wiggled against him, feeling oddly safe and protected in his embrace, even though she could feel his erection against her hip, could literally feel the tension coming off him in waves. He ran one of those big wonderful hands down her back, then settled it against her rump and gave a little squeeze. Like a nitrous button in a racecar, the gentle pressure sent another burst of longing into her already sizzling blood.

Sweet mother, she wanted.

She kissed his neck, then lightly bit and licked the nonexistent wound. She mapped his body with her hands, enjoying the feel of hard muscle, of those impossibly broad shoulders against her hands.

*It would be even better if he were naked,* Viv thought.

The thought, while true, was also sobering. She'd just met him and she'd already crawled into his lap. While she was guilty of all sorts of bad behavior—flipping off the occasional driver, ignoring phone calls from her mother, tearing the Do Not Remove tags from all of her pillows—being a tramp wasn't one of them.

Sexually frustrated and slightly mortified, Viv slowly ended the kiss, then rested her forehead against his. "Hmm. How did I get in your lap?" she asked. "Did you pull me over here or did I climb all over you?"

"Does it matter?"

"Not in the grand scheme of things. I'm just trying to figure out when I became so easy," she said, laughing softly.

"You're not easy. You're into me," he said, obviously pleased with himself. "That just means that you've got very good taste and that you find me irresistible. A man likes that in a woman." Eyes sparkling with humor, he drew back and kissed her again. "But I'm fairly confident that I dragged you over here."

She inwardly breathed a sigh of relief. "Good," she said. "At least I'm not forward."

Hank chuckled. "You crack me up."

"I live to entertain."

Another rumble of laughter. "Somehow I doubt that." He frowned. "You really don't have a Christmas tree?"

*Damn.* She'd said it as a token protest, but had hoped he'd forgotten. "No," she said, expelling a sigh. They were treading into dangerous territory here.

"Change of plans, then. Why don't you choose a tree tomorrow, and I'll bring it by your house tomorrow night. I'll bring dinner. You make cake."

Viv nodded. "That sounds good."

"Sorry I've had to bail on you the past couple of nights," Hank said as dragged a giant tree—not the small one she'd picked out—into her living room via the front door.

Though she'd been deeply disappointed and working at the farm had been a bit lonely without him, Viv merely smiled. "No problem. Duty calls."

And duty had called in the form of his father who'd gone into negotiations with one of the bigger big box stores and had needed his help. What was supposed to have only taken a couple of hours had ended up consuming a couple of days—two of her days with him at the farm. She never thought she'd see the day when she would regret having her community service come to an end, but she did.

Tomorrow was her last day.

Still, Viv had been heartened because he'd called her several times just to talk and they'd logged in hours and hours of conversation. It was pathetic how the simple sound of his voice made her feel like joy was bubbling out of her pores.

Furthermore, she'd gotten quite a bit of work done on his design. As a matter of fact, she had a preliminary mock-up in place and planned to show it to him tonight. For reasons she couldn't explain, she'd yet to deposit his check and book her flight to London. She didn't know why. It was the trip of a lifetime, but despite knowing that she could comfortably afford to take the much anticipated vacation, she couldn't shake the sense that she was just waiting for the other shoe to drop. She inwardly grimaced. Past experience, she supposed.

Hank paused in the middle of her living room and looked around. "Where do you want it?"

"In front of the window, I suppose."

"Is that where you normally put your tree?"

Back to that sticky wicket, were they? "To be honest, I've never had one before."

In the process of loading the tree onto the stand he'd brought, as well, Hank paused, a comically shocked expression on his handsome face. "This is your first Christmas tree?"

"As an adult, yes," she admitted smally, waiting for the fall out. He'd confided on the phone that he'd dumped a girl for using an artificial tree—she couldn't imagine how he would react to knowing that she'd never had a tree—but he had to find out sooner or later and sooner seemed like the better alternative considering…she didn't have any ornaments. He'd mentioned something about his expertise in stringing lights and suspected that he'd come here tonight expecting to trim the tree, as well.

Er…no.

But she *had* made a cake. She smiled brightly. "Would you like a piece of cake?"

"Not before dinner." He settled the tree into the stand and stood back to admire his handiwork, then turned to face her once more. "Are you serious? Are you allergic to evergreen? Do your religious beliefs prevent you from celebrating the holiday?"

"No and no."

"You think it's wasteful to use live trees?"

"Not particularly, no."

Hank frowned. "Work with me here, Viv. What's the problem? He gestured around her living room at her Thanksgiving decorations, which were still proudly on display. "It's obvious you don't have any aversions against decorating. Nice place, by the way," he added as an afterthought.

"Thank you," she murmured.

"So?"

Viv sank onto her couch. She knew this conversation was coming, she'd just been dreading it. He was a Christmas tree farmer and she was a Christmas season hater. At some point, the truth had to come out. Selfishly, she was just hoping that they'd get to make love first.

"Do you remember when I told you that my parents divorced when I was eight?"

He nodded. "I said it when you told me and I'll say it again. Your father sounds like a worthless piece of shit."

Her heart warmed at his outrage on her behalf. "Thank you."

"Anyway—" she blew out a breath "—what I didn't mention was that he walked out on Christmas morning." She swallowed, steepled her fingers against her chin. "It sort of tainted the holiday for me," she said, forcing an uncomfortable smile.

Hank swore. "I reckon that would do it. I'm sorry, Viv. You should have told me. I wouldn't have foisted this tree upon you."

"No," she hastened to tell him. "The tree is beautiful and it's all the more special because you brought it. I'm an adult. I should be able to get over this, right? And on many levels I have, but something about Christmas brings it all rushing back."

"Well, it would, wouldn't it?" he said. He sat down next to her, slung an arm around her shoulder and tugged her up against him.

God, she loved the way she felt when she was in his arms, a little delight she'd gotten to experience again today when they'd snuck off the wood shed for a minute earlier today. Her body, as impossible as it seemed, literally craved him. She ached for him.

"That would be a tough thing to swallow. Eight years old, probably still believing in Santa Claus and your cretin of a father selfishly ruined it for you." He pressed a kiss against her temple. "You know what you need to do, right?"

"What?"

"Make better Christmas memories."

"I've got a few," she said. "I go to my mother's every year. My sister's kids are great. We're still close, you know? Despite what happened. But…"

"Those are memories that someone else is making for you. Your mother's house, your sister's kids. You're a participant, but you're not actively doing anything to change your definition of the holiday. You need to do something for you."

Touched by his concern and impressed with his insight, Viv jerked her head toward the mantle and a ghost of a smile shaped her lips. "I am, actually. See that snow globe?"

"I do."

"That's Hyde Park in London. Provided no disaster strikes and I have to spend the money on something else before I book my ticket, I'm going there this year. The day after Christmas."

"Wow," he said, whistling low. "I've always thought I'd like to go to London. There's a lot of history there. You're going to Stonehenge, right?"

She nodded, wishing that she had the courage to ask him to go with her. Things had moved at warp speed between them, most particularly her feelings. If she had any sense at all, she'd be terrified. As it was, she just wanted him to stay with her. Forever would work.

"I am going to Stonehenge."

"You'll have to tell me all about it when you get back."

Excellent, Viv thought. That implied that he was thinking about them in the short term at least. Her heart gave a little flutter of joy. "I will."

"How long will you be gone?"

"Two weeks," she told him. "I'm going to ring in the New Year over there."

He winced. "Damn. There go my plans."

Her stomach dipped and her gaze swung to his. "What?"

"I was hoping you'd spend New Year's with me."

*Wow.* She smiled, torn, and a nervous laugh tittered up her throat. Trip of a lifetime? New Year with Guy of a Lifetime? "Er…"

"Take your trip," he said, nudging her encouragingly. His intense, slightly hesitant gaze searched hers. "I'll be here when you get back."

It happened right then. She knew because she felt it instantly bud and blossom in her heart, like a magical flower.

Impossibly, against reason, logic and plain old common sense, she fell head over heels in love with Hank Bailey. She'd been hovering since the moment she'd seen him again and now…

She was lost.

Viv leaned over and gently pressed a kiss to his lips. "Stay with me tonight," she said, her voice thick with emotion.

Hank deliberately drew her into his lap and kissed her deeply. Gooseflesh skittered up her spine and settled in the back of her neck. He smiled against her lips. "Why do you think I brought the tree?"

# 8

VIV CHUCKLED against his lips as he picked her up and carried her toward her bedroom. "I thought you were trying to get me into the Christmas spirit." She grinned. "But now I realize you were just trying to get me into bed." She tsked. "That'll put you on the naughty list, you know."

He started down the hall. "Hey, I've been a gold member of the nice club my entire life. I think I'm in better company with you."

Feigning offense, she drew back. "What do you mean 'with you'?"

"You slugged Santa Claus, babe. He might have deserved it, but I'm certain that landed you on the naughty list with Big Red."

She made a thoughtful moue. "I imagine you're right." She tugged his shirt from the waistband of his jeans. "Well, if I'm already on the naughty list, I might as well take advantage of the perks."

Hank laughed. "I'm a perk?" he asked, fishing for the compliment. She tossed his fleece pullover aside and licked a deliberate path up the side of his neck. His breath hissed through his teeth.

"Definitely."

Hank laid her down on the bed, then slid in along beside her. "Ho, ho, ho," he murmured, determinedly snapping each of the three snaps on the front of her shirt.

*Black lace, creamy porcelain skin, a hint of dusky nipple behind the fabric...*

God help him.

Hank traced a gentle swell with his index finger. "You're beautiful. Have I told you that yet?"

A soft smile curled her lips and she cupped his jaw with her small hand. "Many times, thank you. You're not too bad yourself." She released a stuttering breath as he bent and pulled a taut bud into his mouth, suckling her through the fabric. "You make my belly go all hot and muddled. I've been lusting after you since the moment you walked into the gift shop."

"Really?" He liked the sound of that.

She slid her hands over his bare shoulders, measuring his skin against her palms and the contact made a shiver slip up his spine.

"I love your shoulders," she murmured, her voice laced with desire. "I've thought about doing this many, many times." She bent forward and nipped at his shoulder, then carefully licked the spot she'd bitten.

He'd been hard since the moment he'd walked into her door. Impossibly, his dick felt like it had just turned to granite. He winced as equal parts pleasure and pain bolted through him.

He'd wanted to take his time, to take it slow.

Slow wasn't going to be an option, especially if she kept talking to him like that. Viv slid her hand down over his belly and carefully loosened the button on his jeans from its closure. He sucked in a breath as she negotiated the zipper. Half a second later he was in her palm and the breath he'd been holding leaked out of him with a long hiss.

Slow was definitely out of the question.

He needed her naked. Now.

Her shirt landed in the floor with his, her jeans got kicked to the foot of the bed. The matching thong to her bra—also removed—was so pretty he almost decided to leave it on, but one stroke over her weeping mons with his fingers changed his mind.

She worked her hand over his shaft, thumbed the head of his dick, then leaned forward and kissed him again. The kiss was hot and frantic, mimicking sex as her tongue darted in and out of his mouth. He felt a single bead of moisture leak from the head of his penis and knew that he was in serious danger of being finished before they ever official began.

He left her mouth—reluctantly—then kissed a path over each of her breasts and down her sweetly curved belly. She smelled like warm vanilla and musky woman and he was drunk on her scent, hers for the taking.

Hank slipped a finger, parting her curls, then lowered his head between her legs and lapped at her clit.

Gratifyingly, she inhaled sharply and fisted her hands in the sheets. "Hank," she said warningly.

"You taste good," he murmured, licking her deliberately. He slid a finger deep into her channel and hooked it around, looking for that sweet spot that would make her—

She swore and bucked against him.

Ah…there, he thought, smiling against her.

"I'm *so* going to get you back for this," she said, her voice a broken threatening chuckle.

"That's the idea, sweetheart," he said, lapping harder against her.

"Not this way," she said, her breath coming in broken little pants. "I want you inside of me." She tightened around him, her body priming for release. "Please."

As if that was a plea he could refuse. Hank fished a condom from his wallet and swiftly rolled it into place. Three seconds later he was positioned between her thighs, nudging her slickened folds. Her violet gaze tangled with his.

*Cupid's bow lips swollen from his kisses, long curly black hair spread out over a purple satin pillow, puckered nipples pouting for him, her legs open, welcoming him in...*

Something in his chest tightened, then broke apart. He pushed into her...and fell in love.

# 9

VIV WATCHED a series of unreadable emotions flash across Hank's woefully familiar face, then he smiled…and filled her up.

She gasped, drawing her legs back to give him more access. He gritted his teeth as he angled deep. She met him thrust for thrust, could feel the climax ripening in her sex. She was burning up from the inside out, her skin felt too tight for her body and the only thing that mattered in this moment was their connection. She loved the big, hard feel of him. To say that Hank was well-proportioned would be a vast understatement. He was gloriously huge and her body was savoring every, long hardened inch of him.

He bent his head and suckled her right breast again and she winced with pleasure. It felt as though a golden thread ran from the tip of her nipple to the heart of her clit and every tug of his talented mouth coupled with every determined thrust put her that much closer to release.

Viv slid her hands down over his back, tracing the fluted indentation of his spine, then settled her palms over his amazing ass—the one she'd been staring at all week—and gave a squeeze. Gratifyingly, he smiled. "You like my ass?"

"Yeah, but not as much as other parts of you at the moment," she said, writhing against him. She could feel the orgasm building force, circling and circling, but just out of reach. She sank her teeth into her bottom lip and squeezed her feminine muscles around him, trying to hold him longer inside of her.

Hank's grin faded and he upped the tempo, pounding into her. His hardened balls slapped against her aching flesh, the sensation one of the most wonderfully erotic things she'd ever felt.

"Hank, I need—"

He reached between their joined bodies and fingered her clit. She fractured.

*"That,"* she finished in a long keening cry. The orgasm plunged her into pleasure, then lifted her beyond joy. Her release triggered his and with a few more determined thrusts, Hank's big body shuddered above hers.

The idea that she could make this big man quake was one of the most hedonistic things she could have ever imagined.

Viv trailed her fingers along his back, then bent and pressed a kiss against his chest. Hank rolled to her side, quickly disposed of the condom with a napkin from the nightstand, then drew her up next to her. Her head fit perfectly in the crook of his shoulder, as though the space had been divinely designed with her in mind.

He doodled on her upper arm. "Can I tell you something?"

She snuggled closer against him and sighed contentedly, the weight of release making her boneless and rested. "Sure."

"You scare me."

She drew back. "What do you mean?"

"I mean that the first minute I looked at you, I saw a future with you in it."

Though she knew exactly what he meant—she'd had a similar reaction to him, after all—she managed a shaky laugh. "And a future with me is frightening?"

"It is if you're not feeling the same thing I am. It's…intense. I've never been this invested this early in, you know what I mean?"

Boy did she ever. She released a shaky breath. "I do."

"Am I scaring you?"

"Not too much," she admitted. "I'm pretty…invested already, too. More so than I'm used to. Frankly, more than I've ever been. But I've got to tell you, Hank, I've got a history of spooking easily. I've got a bad habit of holding my breath, waiting for something to go wrong. I've always done it."

And it was true. In everything, right down to this airline ticket she had yet to buy. It was awful, really. Why couldn't she just accept things at face value? Why did she always think things would go wrong?

"Forewarned is forearmed," he said, pressing a kiss to her temple. "Just know that if you run away from me, I'll chase you." He gave her a gentle squeeze. "This is special."

Inexplicably tears burned the backs of her eyes. "Even if I hate Christmas?"

"I'll convert you."

Viv chuckled. "You know, I actually think you could."

Hank nuzzled the side of her neck and muttered another suggestive ho-ho-ho. "I should probably start working on that right now," he told her, but before he could complete the promise his cell phone rang.

He drew back and frowned. "Sorry. I'm not expecting a call, but I'd better see who it is." He slipped from the bed and located his jeans, then fished the cell from his pocket. She watched him, lazily admiring his naked form. Dear Lord, the man was beautiful. Dark brown hair over a fabulously muscled chest, flat masculine nipples and a stomach that would make a washboard envious.

And then there was the rest of him.

She swallowed, suddenly hit with the urge to taste him there, to feel that hard hot skin in her mouth.

"It's Brody," he said, a line of concern emerging between his brows.

Viv sat up, her lascivious train of thought derailed. She'd spent a good bit of time with the teenager over the past couple of days and had developed a fondness for the kid.

"Hey," Hank said. He listened, his frown deepening. "Right. Sure. It's no problem at all. I'll be right over. No, no really, I don't mind at all. I told you to call if you ever needed me, didn't I? Stay put. I'll be there to get you in a minute."

Hank disconnected. "I hate to do this, but I've got to leave."

She drew her knees to her chest. "What's wrong?"

"His mother's been gone for the past three days, there's no food in the house and the utilities department has turned off the power." His voice throbbed with anger. "The kid's sitting over there in the dark, hungry and, while he won't admit it, scared. His mother needs her ass kicked," he said, hurrying into his clothes.

Viv completely agreed and would be happy to do the ass-kicking in question. How could a woman treat her child that way? What the hell was wrong with her? "Where's his father?"

"He split when the boy was five. He hasn't seen him since."

Viv's eyes widened significantly. "That certainly sounds familiar." Unbidden an image of her little brother developed in her mind's eye. Dark curly black hair, much like her own. Big blue eyes, much like her own. He'd be about Brody's age, Viv thought now, swallowing. She imagined Brody's sweet smile, that dark hair and blue eyes and her heart began to pound. Dear God… It wasn't possible— It couldn't be…could it?

Her mouth went dry and she had to clear her throat to speak. "Hank, what's Brody's last name?"

He shrugged into his shirt. "Foster. Like yours," he said as though it was just a coincidence.

But it wasn't. She knew it in her heart of hearts, in the very fiber of her soul.

A stifled cry broke from her throat. The poor kid was abandoned, hungry, in the dark and alone. Hands shaking, she scrambled from the bed. "Do you mind if I come with you?"

"No, of course not." His brow furrowed with concern. "Hey, are you all right? You've gone white as a sheet."

Viv took a deep breath. "Hank, I think Brody might be my little brother."

# *10*

"WOW," JASE SAID. "Her brother?"

Hank stood on the porch of the trimming shed as Viv and Brody stood next to her car.

She was leaving, presumably without saying goodbye to him.

Naturally Hank knew that in the grand scheme of things finding a little brother took precedence over telling him goodbye at the moment, but somehow with Viv, he knew it was more than that. She'd been distant with him since last night and he imagined that raking up those old wounds with her father had set her off.

"Yeah," he said. "Small world, isn't it?"

She'd told him about seeing her father with a little boy a few years after her dad had walked out, but that periodic searches in the phone book for his name had been fruitless and she'd just assumed that they'd all moved away. Evidently not. James Foster had moved, but had left another broken family behind.

In Viv's case, their mother was a gem. In Brody's, his mother was a meth addict. The reason that the woman hadn't been home in three days was because she'd been in jail. Luckily, Hank had always had a good rapport with area officials, so getting temporary foster care parent status had been merely a couple of phone calls away. Hank had brought the boy home with him last night.

Last night Viv had confided that at some point in the future she'd like Brody to come and live with her—telling her family was a hurdle, of course—but she knew for the moment that Brody would more than likely prefer to stay with Hank.

Watching the kid's big smile now and the hug he was giving Viv, Hank seriously doubted that. The boy had a family now and instinctively trusted his big sister.

Honestly, the resemblance was striking. He didn't know how any of them had missed it. Same dark hair, same deep blue eyes, same penchant for getting into trouble. He smiled softly. Funny how they'd both ended up here, Hank thought, as though it had been part of some big, cosmic plan.

"You're not just going to let her leave, are you?" Jase asked.

"What do you mean?"

Jase laughed as though he were a moron. "It's obvious you're crazy about her."

He could lie, but what was the point? He merely nodded. "She's special."

"Then don't let her special ass drive away. Go talk to her."

Brody turned to walk away, so Hank made his move. He leapt down from the porch and gave a little holler at Viv. "Hey," he said, loping over. "You're leaving without saying good-bye?"

A forced smile shaped her lips. "I've got to get all this sorted out with Brody," she said, by way of an explanation. It was just as excuse, he knew. "You know, go and talk to my mother and sister. I think that my sister will be as thrilled as I am about him and my mother will accept him into our family because he's a part of us…"

"I imagine it would be hard for her. Brody's the son of the woman your father left her for, right?"

She nodded. "I don't want Mom to be hurt."

"Do you think she knows about him?"

"You know, Dad left without looking back and Mom had to look forward. I'd like to think that if she'd known, she would have told us. But then again she might have thought it would be too painful for us." She lifted a small shoulder. "Having a brother, then not being able to have anything to do with him. I know this—whatever her reason, she had our best interests at heart, which is more than we can say for Brody's worthless waste-of-carbon mother." She smiled at him and touched his sleeve. "Thank you for taking him in. Like I told you last night, I want to talk to my family first— and give him the option—but I'd love for him to come live with me." She smiled and her eyes shimmered with unshed tears. "We're a lot alike, me and Brody."

Hank nodded. "Of course. Just let me know when you're ready." He paused. "Can I see you tonight?"

Her expression froze and a cloud moved behind her gaze. "Er—"

Hank chuckled. "Spooked, are you?"

"I am," she admitted, wincing regretfully. "I just need a little time to sort all of this out, you know?"

He nodded, a bit hurt, but understanding all the same. She'd warned him after all. "I'm not going to stalk you, but I'm not going away, either."

She grinned. "I didn't think you would."

Hank bent and gave her a lingering kiss. If she needed space, he'd give it to her. "Call me when you're ready. I'll be waiting."

It was the noble thing to do, Hank thought. The exact move a guy with Gold Member standing on the Nice list would do…but he'd get Naughty if necessary.

Because there was no way in hell he was losing her.

*I'LL BE WAITING…*

With those words ringing in her ears, Viv got into her car and drove away. He *would* wait, she knew, which was so much more than she deserved considering she'd gone from making love to him to needing a little room. Honestly, she wished there was some way to permanently disengage her self-destruct button. Her life would be so much better if she could.

She'd just found her little brother. She should be celebrating. She should be happy. And she was, truly, at the heart of it all. But all of those issues and insecurities when it came to her father had risen like Lazarus from the dead with this happy news and instead of being able to sort the two out, they were hopelessly intertwined. She was an emotional schizophrenic and Hank Bailey deserved better.

On the surface, Viv was a strong, successful young woman. She knew that. She was proud of her accomplishments, proud of who she'd become. But somewhere deep down inside of her, there was still an abandoned little girl who felt like if her own father couldn't love her, then what man could?

*Hank,* a little voice whispered. *Hank could love you.*

Viv wanted to believe that more than anything in the world. She really did. She wanted to—

Her car suddenly made an ominous sound, then sputtered and died. Black smoke billowed from under the hood as she carefully nursed it to the side of the road.

Viv looked heavenward, then rested her forehead against the steering wheel and laughed darkly as the backs of her eyes burned. Been here, done that, bought the T-shirt.

Predictably, the other shoe had just dropped.

She'd been waiting for it, hadn't she?

A bark of laughter broke loose in her throat as she reached for her cell to phone a tow service. It was a good thing she hadn't bought that plane ticket after all. She'd need the money to fix her car.

Goodbye London.

Goodbye…Hank.

# *11*

*Christmas Eve*

"HAVE YOU HEARD from her?" Jase asked as they closed down for the night.

Hank shook his head. "Not a word."

He'd been patiently waiting for the past week for Viv to come to her senses, but evidently that wasn't going to happen. He knew that, of course, because he knew her. She was afraid of getting hurt, afraid that he'd change his mind, just like her sorry bastard of a father had done. Thankfully he'd kept up with her via Brody who'd talked to her every day. He knew that her car had broken down on her way home last Friday and that she'd spent the money she'd planned on using to go to London on the repairs. It was that damned shoe she was always talking about, Hank thought.

Jase slapped him on the back. "Sorry, bro. I know you had high hopes for this one."

"Who says I don't still have high hopes?"

Jase frowned. "You mean you do?"

He nodded. In fact, he'd already decided on a course of action and was merely waiting until quitting time to put it into action.

Jase blew out a breath, then leaned in as though he were

about to confide something important. "Look, I didn't want to have to tell you this, but I hate to see you make a fool of yourself over nothing."

"What do you mean?"

Jase straightened, seemingly gathering his nerve. "She hates Christmas, Hank. I'm sorry. I didn't want to tell you, but she mentioned it to Mom and Angelica. And considering the way you've been mooning around here all week— Well, I just had to tell you."

Hank laughed. "I knew that already."

Jase's slackjawed expression was priceless. "You knew? Then why are you still pining away? Isn't that a deal breaker?"

He shrugged as though it hardly mattered. And it didn't. "I'll convert her."

"You couldn't convert the artificial-tree girl?" he asked, his voice climbing in shock.

"She wasn't worth the effort."

A slow grin slid over his brother's face and he inclined his head knowingly. "All right, then. Let me know if I can do anything to help."

A thought struck. "As a matter of fact, you can. Could you bag up some ornaments for me and lend me a few strings of Christmas lights?"

Puzzled but willing to help, Jase nodded. "Sure."

Excellent, Hank thought. It was time to get naughty.

SPENT BUT HAPPY that their evening had gone so well, Viv pulled out of her mother's driveway and began the short trek home. Though she'd taken Brody along with her to her family Christmas celebration, her sister Frannie had insisted on taking Brody back out to Hank's herself. Citing all the time that Viv had had with the boy, understandably Frannie wanted to do a bit of catching up. Her brood of nieces and nephews—

all four of them—had been utterly enchanted with the new male addition to the family and had welcomed Brody into their fold with open arms.

Predictably, so had her mother, who had suspected that the child existed, but was never certain. Viv had told her mom her plan to bring Brody into her home and her mother was very supportive. "This will be good. I worry over you being alone," she'd said. "Your sister recovered." Her mom had put her palm on Viv's cheek. "But, despite my best efforts, you never did."

The confession had torn her apart. It had never occurred to Viv that her mother would feel responsible for Viv's inability to truly risk her heart, but she did.

And that was a guilt she couldn't let her mother carry anymore.

Viv made a decision in that instant, one that made her so gloriously happy that she'd literally felt the peace of it slide through her limbs and settle warmly around her heart.

Hank Bailey, the man she loved, was waiting on her.

But he wouldn't be waiting anymore.

Viv planned to go home, wrap a small but significant gift and then go to his house. She knew from Brody that the Baileys traditionally celebrated Christmas tomorrow morning, so with luck she should catch him at home.

She turned onto her street and noticed something strange. She gasped and leaned forward over her steering wheel as she neared her house.

Christmas lights festooned her house. Automated reindeer, snowmen and Santas played music and moved. Fake snow had been sprayed all over her yard and lighted candy canes lined her sidewalk and drive. The bare tree that had stood in her window for the past week was now covered in clear lights and beautiful handmade ornaments.

Most importantly, Hank Bailey sat on her front porch steps, a big smile on his face and a red Santa hat on his head.

Her heart threatening to pound right out of her chest, Viv wheeled the car into her driveway, shifted into Park, then exited the car and made her way up the walk. He stood as she approached and handed her a large red envelope with a foil bow on the corner.

Gray eyes twinkling, he smiled and she thought she'd expire from happiness. "Merry Christmas," he said simply.

"Hank," she breathed.

"This isn't stalking," he said. "This is creating a new Christmas memory."

She chuckled, blinked back tears and looked at everything he'd done for her. "I don't know what to say. It's gorgeous. Thank you."

He smiled and the relief that clung to that grin made her ache for him. He gestured to her gift. "Open it."

She hesitated. "I have something for you, too, but I haven't wrapped it yet. Can we go inside for a minute?"

"Sure."

Hammeringly aware that he was right behind her, Viv hurried into her bedroom, moved a displeased Geraldine from the wrapping paper still on the bed from where she'd tended to the gifts she'd taken to her mother's earlier and snagged a small, empty box. She wrote a note, then placed it inside and quickly wrapped it up.

She found Hank in her living room, admiring the new picture of her and Brody she'd put on the mantle. "You favor each other," he said.

Viv grinned. "I think so, too. I wanted him to know that he's important to me."

Hank turned to look at her. The twinkling lights cast his face in a warm, festive glow. "Oh, I think he knows that."

That left only one person who didn't know how she felt

about them, then. But that was about to change. She handed Hank her "gift."

"Here," she said. "It's not much, but…"

Hank passed her the envelope. "Let's open them at the same time."

She swallowed tightly. "Sure."

Using her fingernail, she carefully opened the envelope and withdrew a stack of papers. It took a full two seconds for her brain to catch up with her eyes and when it did she gasped. "London," she said breathlessly. She looked up just in time to see him read the note she'd placed in the box.

"Your heart?" he said, his voice thick.

"It's not mine anymore," Viv told him. "I just gave it to you."

He smiled then and cleared his throat. "Thank you," he said. "It's the best gift I've ever gotten."

Viv rattled the papers significantly. "This is too much," she said. "I can't let you do this."

Hank sidled forward and wrapped his arm around her waist. "I knew you'd say that, but it's done. Booked, ticketed, ready to go."

"Hank, I don't know what to say. I—"

"Brody told me about your car. I knew you wouldn't go. You and that damned shoe," he said. "We're not waiting on shoes to drop anymore, babe, and if they do, I'll be there to pick it up when it falls." His gaze searched hers. "I love you, Viv."

A lump of emotion swelled in her throat and she leaned forward and kissed his jaw. "I love you, too, Hank."

He drew back. "Besides, there's a catch to your trip, you know?"

"Oh, really? What?"

"If you look closely you'll notice that you're traveling with a guest."

She chuckled softly. "Oh, really? And who would that be?"

"Me." He lifted her off the floor, then kissed her until she couldn't breathe and didn't want to.

Viv smiled against his lips. "Ho, ho, ho," she murmured. "Merry Christmas."

# *Epilogue*

"I HONESTLY DON'T KNOW what we're going to do with you, Damon," his brother droned. Post-season and Santa was soaking his feet, sipping hot cocoa.

Damon blew a smoke ring and smiled even though he was once again on the braided rug, being taken to task for his bad behavior. Pity being bad was so much fun. There was no way in hell he'd ever be able to give it up. Besides, his Christmas had been a happy one, with unexpected results. "You incite Christmas light wars between two neighbors, you sneak sex toys into a fire department toy drive, you—"

"It was a toy drive," he said, blinking innocently. "I happen to like sex toys. You and the missus should give them a try."

His brother released an annoyed sigh. "Children's toys," Big Red emphasized. "It was a *children's* toy drive."

"Why should those snotty little brats have all the fun?" Damon asked. "The adults foot the bill for the occasion. What's the harm in a little sexual gratification at Christmas?" He chuckled darkly. "Trust me, that chick needed a dildo."

"Your evil plan backfired when she actually fell in love, didn't it? All of them, Damon. Every last one of them, even that poor girl you sentenced to the Christmas tree farm found her other half." His brother's shrewd gaze bored into his. "You didn't plan on those people having happy endings, did you?"

Actually, no. He'd thought it would be fun to wind them

up and watch them bounce off one another—not literally, of course. He wasn't a voyeur. He'd thought, at best, they'd all get some great sex for Christmas.

But Big Red was right—each and every one of them had fallen in love. And to his intense surprise, he actually felt…good about that. Pleased even. It wasn't as fun as handing out condoms at FAO Schwartz, but it would do in a pinch.

As a matter of fact, he thought he'd make a yearly habit of this. Steal the list and match up those do-gooders with the not-so-do-gooders. Hell, he might even end up giving that naked little twerp with the bow and arrow a run for his money.

It was a goal, after all, and everybody needed one, right? He blew another smoke ring in the shape of a wreath and grinned, then tossed back another shot of scotch. Santa could have his hot chocolate—Damon needed booze.

*Bestselling author Lynne Graham is back
with a fabulous new trilogy!*

PREGNANT BRIDES

*Three ordinary girls—naive, but also honest and plucky…*

*Three fabulously wealthy, impossibly handsome
and very ruthless men…*

*When opposites attract and passion leads to pregnancy…
it can only mean marriage!*

*Available next month from Harlequin Presents®:
the first installment*

# DESERT PRINCE, BRIDE OF INNOCENCE

\* \* \*

'THIS EVENING I'm flying to New York for two weeks,'
Jasim imparted with a casualness that made her heart sink
like a stone. 'That's why I had you brought here. I own this
apartment and you'll be comfortable here while I'm abroad.'

'I can afford my own accommodation although I may not
need it for long. I'll have another job by the time you
get back—'

Jasim released a slightly harsh laugh. 'There's no need for
you to look for another position. How would I ever see you?
Don't you understand what I'm offering you?'

Elinor stood very still. 'No, I must be incredibly thick
because I haven't quite worked out yet what you're offering
me.…'

His charismatic smile slashed his lean dark visage.
'Naturally, I want to take care of you.…'

'No, thanks.' Elinor forced a smile and mentally willed him not to demean her with some sordid proposition. 'The only man who will ever take *care* of me with my agreement will be my husband. I'm willing to wait for you to come back but I'm not willing to be kept by you. I'm a very independent woman and what I give, I give freely.'

Jasim frowned. 'You make it all sound so serious.'

'What happened between us last night left pure chaos in its wake. Right now, I don't know whether I'm on my head or my heels. I'll stay for a while because I have nowhere else to go in the short term. So maybe it's good that you'll be away for a while.'

Jasim pulled out his wallet to extract a card. 'My private number,' he told her, presenting her with it as though it was a precious gift, which indeed it was. Many women would have done just about anything to gain access to that direct hotline to him, but his staff guarded his privacy with scrupulous care.

Before he could close the wallet, his blood ran cold in his veins. How could he have made such a serious oversight? What if he had got her pregnant? He knew that an unplanned pregnancy would engulf his life like an avalanche, crush his freedom and suffocate him. He barely stilled a shudder at the threat of such an outcome and thought how ironic it was that what his older brother had longed and prayed for to secure the line to the throne should strike Jasim as an absolute disaster....

\* \* \*

*What will proud Prince Jasim do if Elinor is expecting his royal baby? Perhaps an arranged marriage is the only solution! But will Elinor agree? Find out in DESERT PRINCE, BRIDE OF INNOCENCE by Lynne Graham [#2884], available from Harlequin Presents® in January 2010.*

# REQUEST YOUR FREE BOOKS!

## 2 FREE NOVELS
## PLUS 2
## FREE GIFTS!

HARLEQUIN®

*Blaze*™

**Red-hot reads!**

**YES!** Please send me 2 FREE Harlequin® Blaze™ novels and my 2 FREE gifts (gifts are worth about $10). After receiving them, if I don't wish to receive any more books, I can return the shipping statement marked "cancel". If I don't cancel, I will receive 6 brand-new novels every month and be billed just $4.24 per book in the U.S. or $4.71 per book in Canada. That's a savings of 15% off the cover price. It's quite a bargain. Shipping and handling is just 50¢ per book.* I understand that accepting the 2 free books and gifts places me under no obligation to buy anything. I can always return a shipment and cancel at any time. Even if I never buy another book, the two free books and gifts are mine to keep forever.

151 HDN EYS2  351 HDN EYTE

| | |
|---|---|
| Name | (PLEASE PRINT) |
| Address | Apt. # |
| City | State/Prov. | Zip/Postal Code |

Signature (if under 18, a parent or guardian must sign)

Mail to the **Harlequin Reader Service:**
**IN U.S.A.:** P.O. Box 1867, Buffalo, NY  14240-1867
**IN CANADA:** P.O. Box 609, Fort Erie, Ontario  L2A 5X3

Not valid to current subscribers of Harlequin Blaze books.

**Want to try two free books from another line?**
**Call 1-800-873-8635 or visit www.morefreebooks.com.**

\* Terms and prices subject to change without notice. Prices do not include applicable taxes. N.Y. residents add applicable sales tax. Canadian residents will be charged applicable provincial taxes and GST. Offer not valid in Quebec. This offer is limited to one order per household. All orders subject to approval. Credit or debit balances in a customer's account(s) may be offset by any other outstanding balance owed by or to the customer. Please allow 4 to 6 weeks for delivery. Offer available while quantities last.

**Your Privacy:** Harlequin Books is committed to protecting your privacy. Our Privacy Policy is available online at www.eHarlequin.com or upon request from the Reader Service. From time to time we make our lists of customers available to reputable third parties who may have a product or service of interest to you. If you would prefer we not share your name and address, please check here.

HB09R3

# COMING NEXT MONTH

## Available December 29, 2009

**#513 BLAZING BEDTIME STORIES, VOLUME III** Tori Carrington and
Tawny Weber
*Bedtime Stories*
What better way to spend an evening than cuddling up with your better half,
indulging in supersexy fairy tales? We guarantee that sleeping will be the last
thing on your mind!

**#514 MOONSTRUCK** Julie Kenner
Claire Daniels is determined to get her old boyfriend back. She's tired of
being manless, especially during the holidays, and she'd like nothing more than
a New Year's Eve kiss to start the year off right. And she gets just that. Too bad
it's not her ex-boyfriend she's kissing…

**#515 MIDNIGHT RESOLUTIONS** Kathleen O'Reilly
*Where You Least Expect It*
A sudden, special kiss between two strangers in Times Square on New Year's
Eve turns unforgettable, and soon Rose Hildebrande and Ian Cumberland's sexy
affair is smokin' hot despite the frosty weather. Will things cool off, though, once
the holiday season ends?

**#516 SEXY MS. TAKES** Jo Leigh
*Encounters*
It's New Year's Eve in Manhattan and the ball is about to drop in Times
Square…. Bella, Willow and Maggie are on their way to the same blockbuster
Broadway audition until fate—and three very sexy men—sideline their journey
with sizzling results!

**#517 HER SECRET FLING** Sarah Mayberry
Don't dip your pen in the office ink. Good advice for rookie columnist
Poppy Birmingham. Too bad coworker Jake Stevens isn't listening. Their recent
road trip has turned things from antagonistic to hedonistic! He wants to keep
this fling on the down-low…but with heat this intense, that's almost impossible.

**#518 HIS FINAL SEDUCTION** Lori Wilde
Signing up for an erotic fantasy vacation was Jorgina Gerard's ticket to
reinventing herself. The staid accountant was more than ready for a change, but
has she taken on too much when she meets and seduces the hot, very gorgeous
every-woman-would-want-him Quint Mason? She's looking forward to finding out!

**www.eHarlequin.com**

HBCNMBPA1209